# A SHIELD FOR ESTUARIUS

# A Shield for Estuarius

---

## *yet another problem for mom*

**TAIRY DIAZ GIL**

# CONTENTS

To my husband who supports all my harebrained ideas, and
to my children who show me the magic of every day.

*Joseph... that should help him find my dead body, if he can find something without me that is... How's Doggie going to escape this assailant? His leash is tied around my waist!* – Taking a deep breath to center her emotions, she rose slowly, pretending to knot the bag, and ready to smear the steaming offer right onto the threat's face – *I am not going to go down easy!*

A shadowed figure was standing a few steps away from Doggie, right out of the reach of his leash. The figure was tall and lean and the air around it seemed to be alive in the shimmer of heat. Eliane just stared at the visitor, waiting for their next move, holding onto the unknotted bag as if her life depended on it.

"Is that... is that a miniature poodle or a standard?" Asked the figure, coming out of the shadows with a big smile on his face.

"He is a tall mini" Responded Eliane, still unsure whether this man was a threat but noticing that Doggie had stopped growling, and it was now sitting, waiting quietly.

"Hello handsome" he said while kneeling down on the ground, still out of reach from the dog.

"His name is Doggie" Eliane had relaxed a bit, noticing that it would be harder for the stranger to do anything from his position.

"Hello Doggie, my name is Gary. Can I give him a treat?" He asked, reaching for a pocket in his black leather jacket – *why is he all dressed in black at night? Cars won't be able to see him when he's crossing the street!*

"No!" The apprehension came back full force until he

stopped going for his pocket, bringing his hands back in front of him. "He is allergic to certain ingredients" she explained.

"I get it. He is beautiful" he continued to just kneel there, giving space to the dog but not making full eye contact with him.

"Yes, yes he is" she absolutely agreed with him.

"May I pet him?" He asked with a smile. He had a nice smile, she noticed, it reached all the way to his dark eyes.

"If he allows it, you may touch him under the chin."

Eliane knew that Doggie wasn't the biggest fan of men. Normally, if a man showed up when they were walking alone, he would bark up a storm and not allow them to get near her. But now, it was different, he had been sitting quietly and content and very few people have ever been deserving of his patience. Noticing how quiet and at ease he was, Eliane couldn't help but relax, trusting her dog's instincts but still not willing to let go of her odorous weapon.

To Eliane's surprise, Doggie started wiggling his whole body and showing all the signs of excitement and affection that he reserved for the people he knew well. "Well, it seems he likes you!"

"I'm honoured" And he seemed to mean it, he was petting his neck and behind the ear while telling him he was a good boy with that voice that most people reserve for babies and dogs.

Somehow, she found herself walking alongside the stranger – *what was his name? He had mentioned it* – and was ok with it. They struck a conversation where he said he had recently arrived, and that the area had changed so much since his last visit.

"Oh yeah, we have only been here a bit over a decade and it's completely different now. All that over there used to be farmland" Eliane replied, pointing to her left.

They continued chatting about nothing in particular when he stopped. She had taken a few steps before noticing that he was no longer walking beside her. She turned to see where he was and made a gesture as if to ask him if there was something wrong. "I don't quite know how to say this without sounding like a lunatic" he commented.

"Try me" Eliane said curiously.

"I know your lineage and I need something from you" he declared, looking at her.

Cursing herself from lowering her guard – *they say it in the true crime podcast, the gals ALWAYS say it in the podcast!* – she racked her mind to find a new weapon but didn't dare to take her eyes off him – *remember: yell, don't scream, that is what they always say: yell, don't scream... What the heck is the difference? Why didn't I research the difference? I'm going to effing DIE because I do not know the difference between yelling and screaming!*

"I come from a different reality that is within your world and only your blood can save us" Eliane barely heard him over the turmoil in her head.

"Go on..." She replied slowly – *keep this lunatic talking; the longer he talks the bigger the chances someone will walk by before he takes all my blood. And why, oh why is Doggie being so happy smelling that tree? Instead of being on alert? Have a dog, they say... bark you happy mop, bark!*

"There is magic in our reality, but it gets poisoned by your technology." The stranger continued his explanation in the same tone someone would use to tell you the sky is blue. "Your ancestors come from our reality. They adapted and evolved. Your blood is immune to electronics, it's the perfect link between our worlds."

"Interesting" – *Maybe I can get my phone. How is it that you can reach 911 without actually calling? Was it by shaking it? Do I have to press the side buttons a bunch of times? Why am I so flipping ignorant?! This is what happens when you don't know squat, a lunatic takes all your blood and leaves your dog attached to your dead waist and they smell your ear for an hour while your murderer escapes!*

"Yes! I just need you to come with me" The stranger cheered at Eliane's apparent positive reaction.

"I would need to drop Doggie off first" she said to buy herself some time.

"I guess you would need to tell Joseph too" he said matter-of-factly.

Eliane froze. This guy just mentioned her husband by name. She hadn't said his name during the walk. She was more careful than that, she knew she had not revealed any personal details – *this is not random. I'm being targeted. Is he a serial killer? Has she heard about any women drained of blood in the area? Maybe if she actually read the news she would know! –*

All of the sudden she felt calm wash over her, the jig was up, there was no point in pretending anymore.

"I see you are name dropping now" she said calmly while unbuckling the leash from her waist – *I will give Doggie a chance to escape this. I'll be damned if I didn't at least save my dog!*

"What are you doing?" he sounded slightly worried at her change in demeanor.

"I'm not going to make it easy for you to exsanguinate me." She was now holding the leash on her hand; she was sure that throwing the metallic end at his face would buy her at least 30 seconds.

"Exsanguinate you?!" he said, sounding surprised "I only need one drop of blood at the Arch of Renewal!"

"The what, now?" confusion again, this was proving to be quite the rollercoaster of a conversation.

"The Arch of Renewal… wait, did you really think I was going to drain all your blood? Do you think I'm a human killer?!" he started to sound panicked.

"Well yes, aren't you?" – *a HUMAN killer? what the heck?*

"By the Belt, this can't be happening!" he was pacing nervously now.

"What…? What belt?" she asked, confused and curious.

"Oh my" he paused, took a deep calming breath and continued "The Belt is the part where our realities connect. Imagine a clear sphere with a ball inside of it. When you swirl the clear sphere, the ball inside also swirls and it does so always in contact with the sphere. The clear ball represents Earth, and that swirl is its movement around its own axis.

The smaller ball inside of it is Estuarius, and it's in a different reality that most humans are not aware of.

"Woah" Eliane exhaled. Against her better judgment, she was simply fascinated by the stranger's delusion. She had always had a soft spot for anything related to fantasy.

"Ok, so you haven't seen magic in the human world because technology, specifically the waves all around us, blocks it. Why do you think there were so many unexplained phenomena before the technology boom?"

"Air waves? Like microwaves and Bluetooth?" Eliane asked.

"YES!" he said excitedly "There used to be more of a flow between our realities before the invention of electricity. Have you heard a hum when you walk by electricity towers?" as Eliane nodded, he continued "That hurts magic. Why do you think Scotland's national animal is the unicorn? You think a country would just use an imagined animal? No, some came to Earth through the Belt. You'll see them around when we cross."

"But why would I go with you? I have responsibilities, a life, people that depend on me." Eliane wasn't sure when she started believing him, but she knew he was speaking the truth. This was real.

"Listen, it doesn't have to be you, it just needs to be someone that shares your blood, someone in your nucleus. I can ask Leo if he'd help." He explained.

"My oldest son is 9, I'm not going to put him in a train and send him away to fight a guy without a nose!" she said in shock.

"What? Nobody is fighting anyone with or without noses,

whatever that means. All you have to do is stand under the Arch of Renewal, spill one tiny drop of blood, and the magic in your blood will activate and renew the protection spells for another 106 Earth years. Clarissa did it without a problem last time and went back to her nucleus without any issues."

"Clarissa? You mean my great grandmother? Did you meet her?" Eliane was fascinated.

"Oh yes, she was all business and didn't accept any nonsense around her" he said with a smile, recalling fond memories.

"How long will we be gone?" She was slightly surprised that she had accepted but it felt right.

"Oh, I doubt it would be more than 2 Earth hours" he said, happy now that Eliane agreed to the trip.

"Earth hours?" there were just too many variables for Eliane to keep up.

"Yes, remember the ball within the clear sphere? It spins faster so time there is faster compared to time here, 1 hour on Earth is 24 hours in Estuarius. Thus, 15 minutes is 6 hours, 5 minutes is 2 hours, and 2.5 minutes an hour.

If Eliane had needed any extra convincing, the math would have cemented her decision. Not only did she love mathematical explanations, but she also wouldn't really be gone for long.

"It all sounds so simple" she said like it was an everyday thing that someone explains how there's a whole new reality that they can access with a small time distortion.

"It really is! Nothing could go wrong" he exclaimed with a big smile.

"Don't say that" – *all I need is for this guy to jinx it!*

"Why not?" the man looked so confused, it was almost laughable.

"Because those are famous last words!" she explained, a little exasperated.

"Really? By whom?"

Without knowing how to respond to that, she sighed and said "Ok, I'll go, can't wait to meet Legolas!"

"Who?" the confusion just kept on increasing on his face.

"Never mind. But for real this time, I need to leave Doggie at home and tell my husband what's going on" she explained.

"Are you going to actually tell him about Estuarius?" they started walking once more, the confusion replaced by surprise.

"Well yeah, I'm married to him, and he needs to know where I am."

"But… just come" he pleaded.

"Listen, if I'm going anywhere, I will tell him first. It's the responsible thing to do and it will make me feel safer." She wasn't going to take no for an answer.

# | 2 |

# Out Of Reality

Once she made it home, Eliane thought it would be safer if the stranger stayed outside – *I should really figure out his name* – She found Joseph leaning on the kitchen counter, watching videos on his device while the kids were upstairs getting ready for bed.

"Honey?" she said while embracing him and resting her head on his back.

"What's up?" he replied while pausing the video and turning around to face her.

Normally, you couldn't read Joseph's face, but anyone could have easily seen how his eyes kept getting bigger and bigger as Eliane told him about the encounter. He was not impressed with her at all.

"Honey," Joseph had to take a deep breath before continuing. "I know you like fantasy and all your weird books, but that is not an Aes Sedai waiting for you out there. That is a human being having a psychotic episode and we need to

**11**

call 911" said Joseph with eyes as big as they could go. He was holding her arms pinned to her sides, fingers digging uncomfortably in her skin, desperately trying to put some sense into her.

"Babe, I know, I know that but…"

"Do you?!" he interrupted her forcefully, letting go of her arms, and combing his fingers through his hair as he paced back and forth, back and forth "You are just going to leave us? Do you even read the news? Don't answer that. Do you have *any* idea about what happens every day? What are the kids going to do without their mom? How do I explain away your disappearance?"

"Honey, I won't be gone for long!" she said appeasingly.

"That is what he is saying" he interrupted exasperated "and you are believing him. You don't even know his flipping NAME!"

"Yes, she does." Said a calm and unexpected voice.

Eliane and Joseph turned around to see the stranger standing by the kitchen door. The air around him looked both diminished and alive with movement. Joseph immediately moved in front of Eliane to shield her with his body "call 911", he ordered briskly.

"She knows my name is Gary. I told her." He said calmly, matter-of-factly.

"Get out of my house" Joseph's words sent a chill down Eliane's spine. She had never heard Joseph use that tone before. It was low and threatening, a sound that promised violence and pain.

"I didn't want to do anything, but you are not leaving me

any choice" Gary made a dismissive motion with his hand, like the gesture someone might do when shooing a fly from one's face. Joseph, startled, stood very rigidly, arms pinned to his sides, legs closed tightly together, unnaturally.

"What did you do to my husband?!" Eliane whisper shouted. She did not want the kids to hear the commotion and come downstairs to investigate whatever this was.

"I just stopped him so he can listen. It won't last long, especially not under these fluorescent lights. The magic will dissolve very fast" Gary explained.

Eliane was speechless, trying to comprehend what was happening. Her husband looked for all the world that he was completely tied with invisible rope. She didn't know what to say so she said nothing while alternating her gaze between Gary and Joseph.

"Everything is true. There's no technology that can do what I just did to you. You know that" Gary said soothingly.

Joseph stopped struggling and listened.

"All those stories, all those things you can't explain come from somewhere. They come from my world, from Estuarius." He continued explaining calmly. "When the Belt gets thinner, sometimes ripples of our magic come out in waves toward Earth and that affects everyone. You have seen its effects; you even have a name for it. Humans call it the Mandela Effect".

At this, Joseph visibly relaxed. He always found it fascinating how so many people could misremember something so specific and in the exact same way.

"If the Belt collapses," Gary continued, "nobody can tell what the onslaught of magic can do to Earth but I can assure you that Estuarius will die, poisoned by all the electronic waves that will pass through. Millions of people will die. Animals, plants, and even buildings would crumble! Some will simply cease to exist, others will be poisoned and slowly disintegrate just like your ropes did a few seconds ago," he said, nodding his head towards Joseph as if to emphasize his words.

"Is it even safe for her to go?" he asked in a low voice, looking at his wife with the worried expression that can only come from love. Eliane noticed he didn't seem to be tied up anymore.

"Yes, her family has been doing it for many generations" Gary declared.

"I don't know..." Joseph looked defeated when he said this, his head hanging low, looking at his own feet.

Gary moved slowly toward Joseph "you don't need to know; you just need to trust your wife. Do you trust her?"

"I... I do. I don't understand any of this, but I believe it and I trust you" Said Joseph turning to look at his wife "are you going to say bye to the kids before you go?"

With a content smile on her face, Eliane kissed her husband on the cheek "Yes, I'll go upstairs and pray them good night" and she left the two men in the kitchen.

* * *

Without a sound, a silver line appeared in mid air, suspended above the grass in the middle of the field. The line was just there for a whole breath as if it had always existed. Suddenly, it started to pulsate, slowly at first, then gaining speed until it seemed to be vibrating so fast, it was but a blur. It was at this point that it seemed to open, like a rift in time itself. A portal from Earth had opened.

* * *

If Eliane had been standing in front of the portal that brought her to Estuarius, she would have seen how one of her legs was seemingly coming out of a wall of pure silver. She was too stunned trying to take in the alien view to notice Gary standing next to her until he exclaimed "What in the Blood…? This is not the right place" The tall man was looking up at the dark green foliage and the long purplish fruits hanging from the trees.

"What?!" Eliane's shrill and loud question made several blue and yellow birds take flight.

"Please lower your voice, several hunting things may want to have a taste" Gary urged in a whisper.

Eliane repeated her question but this time she did so in an angry whisper "what do you mean that this is not the right place?"

"Nothing, nothing, I just need to figure out where we are." He said calmly.

"What do you mean?" Eliane was working really hard on controlling her mounting panic. She had just stepped through a rant in the air at the end of her driveway. She had done so under the sure knowledge that she was coming to this unknown place for only a couple of minutes – *Earth minutes!* – She knew she was going to be back in time to put her boys to bed, she just knew it but this… this negated that knowledge. This brought uncertainty as to when she was going to be back to them – *what have I done?*

"Just checking." He exclaimed dismissively.

"Explain yourself" she urged – *did I just leave my children without a mom?* – tears were starting to accumulate at the bottom of her eyes while she wrung her hands in quiet despair.

"Maybe if you stop hyperventilating in my ear and spitting words between your teeth, I can concentrate enough to figure out what the Dry Dirt is happening and then I can explain it to you, ok?!"

Taken aback by the hissed outburst, Eliane blinked away her unshed tears, took a deep breath, and decided to focus her attention on studying her surroundings. The tall dark green conical trees would not have felt amiss on Earth except for the fact that pine trees do not have purple fruits, nor do they have small white flowers. It seemed to be the middle of the day as the sun was right above them making their shadows just dark puddles under their feet.

After what seemed like an eternity, but it was really just a few short minutes, Gary explained that they landed in a place way off, and that it would take about two days to get to where they were supposed to be.

"Everything will be fine, don't worry" he said with a smile.

"What about the hunting things you mentioned?" Eliane kept looking around, expecting a 3-headed animal to jump out from behind a tree.

"They will be fine. We just need to make sure they do not put us on their menu. Please don't touch any giant flowers, or anything that may look cute and fuzzy. Let's get some water and food for the trek ahead." He said while walking towards a silver ravine behind Eliane – *My kids will be fine; they will just have to miss me a couple more hours than I thought. I hope Joseph doesn't worry too much.*

"And so, it begins" she muttered while falling into step behind Gary.

Gary produced several pouches from between his jacket and filled them up with the cold water of the ravine. He also produced a piece of waxed fabric where he lined up a few plants taken from the ravine slope. "These plants will keep us well fed for days. They are not the tastiest but at least we won't be lacking nutrients. We'll grab some fruits from the trees on our way to town."

Eliane nodded silently and collected what was given to her. She thanked the fact that she was wearing joggers instead of her usual yoga pants – *small pockets so I can carry my food is better than no pockets at all!* – Gary kept all the water as Eliane had nowhere to stash it.

"Please keep an eye out for little yellow flowers, they look like a little ball and have tiny white ends. We need their leaves come the morning" Gary instructed.

"Sure. More super plants to keep us strong?" she asked.

"Not at all. They are called 'Morning Leaves' and it's important to chew them in the morning to avoid mouth rot and to give us nice breath. They normally have them as a paste at shops in town so you can rub it on your teeth, but just chewing them will have the same effect" Gary sounded like a proud boy scout.

"How am I going to be able to speak to people?" she asked while scanning the ground for the yellow flowers.

"The same way you are doing it right now" replied Gary in confusion.

"You mean they also speak English? Like you?" Eliane asked surprised yet excited – *what are the odds?! That only ever happens in the movies.*

"What is 'English'?" he asked with the awkward way people have when pronouncing a strange word for the first time.

"The language we are speaking" – *duh!*

"Oh no, no, no, we are each speaking our own language, your brain is translating simultaneously, it's an effect of the Belt. It lets each reality understand the other one."

"Oh, like the Tardis" the complete and utter confusion on his face almost made Eliane laugh.

"The Tar... whatever, yes, like the Tardis" he sighed, unable to comprehend what Eliane was talking about but satisfied that she seemed to understand the concept.

As they continued the trek to their original landing place, Eliane studied her surroundings in silence. There seemed to be the same types of animals that she would expect to see in a place like this back home. However, they were slightly different, mostly where it came to their colors. There were birds with all sorts of combinations: yellow and blue, violet and orange, deep purple and red, even one that was green, pink, and orange! Some creatures looked like monkeys, they had orange fur with reddish fingers but two tails. She noticed green, blue, and grey squirrels. And she was sure she spotted a snake that seemed to have brown polka dots all over its green body.

They picked fruits as they walked. The long purple ones that looked like a light eggplant, burst into sweet juice when Eliane took a bite, and the little red pear-like with big seeds, tasted the way roses smell back home.

As far as adventures went, this one seemed like a fun, yet unprepared for, camping trip so she enjoyed the hike and eating from nature.

When night came, Eliane worried about sleeping directly on the ground. She felt that she was of an age where any minor inconvenience left her aching the following day. She even remembered having hip pain for almost a whole day from having slept on top of the border of a towel once. She should not have worried. She was in Estuarius, a land of magic and wonder. Gary made movements as if fluffing up some pillows that left her space soft and comfortable. Within seconds of testing the comfort she fell into a deep restorative sleep.

* * *

It was nice walking the familiar streets again. Eliane didn't remember walking these since she was in high school, and she was finally allowed to go home on foot by herself. She thought that things felt a bit empty but she shook the feeling out, closed her eyes, and turned her face upwards to feel the sun on her skin – *why can't I hear the birds?* – she opened her eyes again and looked around, with a content smile on her face and the happy feeling of tasting independence for the first time – *mom will let me use the city bus by myself soon* – She kept on walking and thought of an old friend – *JB used to live around here, yes, it was nice when he took me to see the Nutcracker. It was his first year of university. It was nice to ride in a car driven by a friend instead of my mom... I should go say hi* – She looked around, she remembered his building being square and white. She saw it, it was easy to spot the yellow form amid all the houses. The building looked a bit strange without glass in its windows. She turned around to see what the blue light was she had seen from the corner of her eye, but she couldn't see anything, it must have been her imagination. She turned back and walked to the building where she knew her friend was waiting, the sun reflecting in the windows made her squint.

She couldn't remember which apartment JB lived in. Maybe if she started going up, she would remember – *how am I going to go upstairs? The door to the stairs is always locked* – she walked deeper into the building, it was very dark – *maybe the lobby light is broken* – she could see something on her right, so she walked towards it, it was the staircase! The wide grey steps seemed somehow inviting, she took one step, then another. Everything looked so dark, the wood paneling on the walls seemed to swallow the little illumination that was about. Eliane got a bad feeling – *is that a blue light?* – she decided to go back down to the lobby.

"I know his apartment" there was a smiling woman in the lobby. She was middle aged, with short salt and pepper hair, she could had easily been Eliane's mom.

"You do?" Eliane asked excitedly, she really wanted to say

hi to JB. It had been so long; they were good friends. Maybe they could hang out at the bakery in the corner.

"Yes, it's on the first floor" the smiling woman said while pointing towards the staircase with her head.

"But the stairs… They are too dark. I don't like it" Eliane said while rubbing her arms as if cold.

"That's ok, look, his older brother is here" In walked a tall muscular man, blue eyes, clean-shaven, angular jaw. When he saw her, he smiled, and Eliane saw he had gorgeous white teeth and a little dimple formed on his left cheek.

Eliane felt a rush of blood go to her face "hi…" she said almost out of breath.

"Hi! Long time without seeing you!" His smile widened and he gave her a long tight hug. She felt enveloped in the strength, and she closed her eyes to smell the scent of him. She felt dizzy and warm. She was filled with disappointment when he let go of her "Come upstairs!" With a hand on her back, he guided her back towards the stairs.

She was lying down on a soft mattress, with a book on her lap. She felt him entering the well-lit room through the door that was by her head. He went directly to the closet in front of her. He was only wearing boxers, she could see the shape of his broad back and his muscular legs – *I should read this book, I don't want him to catch me looking at him* – she looked down at her book, but she couldn't concentrate, one letter seemed to be bright blue – *R* – she stole another glance. He was wearing jeans, and his back was still turned towards her, she could see the muscles on his arms flexing as he unfolded a white shirt. His head was slightly turned, and she felt that the sharp angle of his jaw was calling out to her. She turned another page in the book and glanced towards it to pretend to be reading it – *U* – but she couldn't stop her eyes from wandering up to see him. He was wearing dark pants and a crisp white shirt and, more importantly, he was looking at her with a smile that made her heart skip a beat. He said, "shall we?" She briefly looked down at her book to make sure she had closed it properly – *was that an N?*

He was covering the one window that gave the room light. She thought of JB – *why would I think of JB? He moved to a different country and had two kids with his wife, right?* – she was going to ask him but got distracted with that little bit of skin she could see picking out from under his shirt when he lifted his arms over his head to reach the curtains. She could hear her blood pounding on her ears.

Sitting next to him at the fountain felt right. The seat was hard, but the softness of his skin distracted her. The lake at their feet was dark, she couldn't see the bottom. It was night-time but she could see him, all she could see was him. Nothing else mattered. He saw her looking at him and moved ever so slowly towards her. Her heart accelerated and she tilted her head just so and shifted her eyes to look at the darkness over the water, trying to appear inviting, yet detached. She could feel his warm breath on her neck when he leaned towards her and whispered, "listen to the music with me, you want to listen to it with me" She leaned towards him, still looking at the darkness, she was trying her best to listen to the music coming from his earbud. The hot breath at her ear made her shudder. He brushed the skin of her neck ever so softly with his lips "listen with me" he whispered invitingly. She shuddered again, her mouth parted, and she leaned more, her eyes started to close – *JB doesn't have an older brother!* – her eyes flew open, and she froze. Her sudden stiffening made his earbud fall to the ground. She went to her knees to look for it, but something was wrong. She scanned her surroundings; all she could see was the cold tiles of the fountain – *where's the earbud? He is going to be so mad if I can't find it!* – she kept scanning, scanning, her shoulder started to feel warm, so she looked at it, there was nothing wrong with it, but it was oh so warm, like a fever. She saw a blue light over her shoulder. There was something in the water, yes, she could see something blue and bright coming towards her, no, not towards her but in her direction, it was going to pass her by. It looked like a bright serpent head – *a dragon* – she smiled and reached towards it. She has always loved dragons. Her shoulder was so hot, it was starting to hurt. Behind her, she could hear him calling to her, calling her in a whisper, calling to listen, to listen to the music. She wanted to turn towards him, to see his eyes, to listen to whatever he wanted her to listen, but she needed to touch the bright blue dragon head under the surface of the water... if she could just touch it... she stretched towards it...

* * *

Eliane opened her eyes to the forest night filled with stars. Gary moved his hand off her shoulder, softly saying "you are safe now, sleep". Eliane turned to her side and was immediately asleep.

* * *

Eliane opened her eyes at first light. Everything around her seemed to be awake, she could hear the birds welcoming the new day. Gary gave her a pouch of water while she chewed her morning leaves. They had fresh fruits for breakfast and Gary produced tea from one of his pockets to wash it all down. When their modest but filling meal was over, they packed camp and started that day's march. They were halfway through the morning when Eliane started having that telling stomach feeling that she had been dreading since Gary told her it would take them two days to reach their original destination.

She tried to tough it up and kept on walking. If she just ignored it, it would just go away, right? She started sweating while getting cold chills all over her body, she simply could not leave it any longer.

"Gary?" She called, prepared to swallow her pride.

"Yes?"

"I need to go behind those bushes for some privacy" she said vaguely, hoping he would understand without having to say anything more.

"Ok, I'll brew us some tea while we wait."

"But... Gary?" *Please don't make me say it!*

"Yes, Eliane?"

"I... I don't have toilet paper" she blurted.

Gary just stared blankly at her.

"Please don't make me repeat it" if there was a moment she was regretting coming into this adventure, this was it.

"Oh, I heard you, I just don't understand" he said, waiting for clarification.

"I need something to… to wipe my butt" she said, face burning with red heat.

Gary burst out laughing with realization, "just take some of those big leaves. You'll be much cleaner squatting than sitting. Here" he gave her one of the clear water pouches he carried in his person "just in case."

Red faced, Eliane walked to the trees far enough so he couldn't hear Gary laughing anymore – *that should be far enough that he won't hear anything embarrassing, oh God I hope nothing bites me while I squat! This is why I only go camping where there's bathrooms!*

* * *

They finally arrived where they were originally destined. Two stone arches in the middle of a green field.

"This is an entrance to the belt that touches Earth, we have been walking along the Belt all this time." Gary explained while looking at the stone arches "There are only 3 of these entrances. These 3 points are where the Belt is thinnest between our realities so travel through is easiest. Being this close to the Renewal must be weakening things and I think that is why the portal must have dropped us on the wrong spot."

If Eliane had been watching Gary instead of studying the arches, she would have noticed him knitting his eyebrows. He was looking at something that seemed to be embedded between the vines that creeped all over the arches. He reached and grabbed something from between the leaves, put it in one of his many deep pockets, and continued as if nothing uncommon had occurred.

They walked just a few more hours to Mossbrook, the nearest town where they would prepare to go to the Arch of Renewal.

# | 3 |

# A New Reality

After about an hour of walking, Eliane could see buildings in the distance.

"That's Mossbrook" said Gary when he noticed Eliane gazing at the distant structures.

"It looks so modern. Those buildings could belong to any city of Earth."

"We have been evolving for many years, Eliane. We have civilizations and modern structures. What did you expect?" he asked, perplexed.

"Honestly? I don't know. You said you don't have technology so maybe I pictured something out of a medieval movie. I don't know."

"Not having electricity does not mean not having technology. It's just not automated the way your cities are. We also have plenty of magic, remember?" he said with a kind smile and a wink.

After a while, they arrived at the small town. It really

looked like any town back home, except there were no cars, no light posts, no billboards, and it was definitely lacking the smell of smog. Instead, there were several clear tubes going from building to building, supported in the air by tall posts covered in vines. There were trees everywhere and all the buildings seemed to have vines on the sides. Everywhere she looked, she could see greenery and flowers. And that is when she finally noticed the people.

Simply put, everyone was beautiful. Nobody seemed to be particularly tall, but their features were so elegant, their walk so graceful, that they seemed to be taller. It could have been anywhere on Earth; they all looked human enough, some were taller than others, heavier than others, and lighter than others. They all had big round eyes that made them look like someone had drawn them. It was hard not to stare, some had skin as white as porcelain and some skin so dark that it almost shone blue. Most of them had sort of a golden hue to their skin.

Everyone seemed to glide instead of walk, like dancers. It could had been their clothing. Most were wearing dresses and flowy pants, their clothes looked both comfortable and practical.

As they continued to walk, she noticed that there seemed to be patches of farmland between buildings at regular intervals. The clear tubes she had seen before split into many more over these patches of land and seemed to create a spiderweb above the crops "What are those over the planting?"

"That's the irrigation system. There is a big pipe on the other side of town that feeds us water directly from the sea. It arrives to the water processing plant where it gets de-salted and then most of the freshwater is sent to the Capital and neighboring towns. The rest is carried all over Mossbrook through all the clear tubes you see. Some go underground to feed the buildings. The ones above ground collect the sunlight and reflect it back at night. It's quite beautiful!"

Eliane had stopped walking, trying to absorb it all "you are telling me that you get the water from the oceans and use it to feed the town? Is that the same all over Estuarius?"

"Of course," Gary replied, "Our planet is mostly comprised of ocean water, it just makes sense to use it."

Eliane shook her head and laughed "this is paradise! I love it here!"

Gary swelled with pride, and they resumed their walk "let's see what news the day brings" he said, walking purposely to a squat green building. "This is the place to find anything we need."

"Good tidings Guider, we thought you lost by the Dust Raiders!" Said a short golden man with ruby hair as soon as they came into the building.

"Peace, Shop Keeper. We are here without a scratch, just a simple delay. What is this mention of Dust Raiders?" Gary asked, looking worried.

"They have been attacking all caravans and is rumored that Tech Golems are among their ranks."

"I don't like the sound of this. How accurate are your news, Shop Keeper?"

"I won't take offence at your question, Guider, as I know you are worried about the Renewal" the golden man said, clearly taking offense.

"Peace. I apologize for expressing words without thought.

I would feel better if word was sent to the Capital. A security detail would be more than appreciated on our way to the Arch of Renewal. We must not allow Dust Raiders to interfere with the Renewal. Could you arrange this?"

"It will be done as commanded, Guider" the Shop Keeper bowed his head and remained bowed as Gary and Eliane exited the shop.

Once outside, Gary turned to Eliane and explained "We'll have to wait a few days for a protection group to come and escort us to the Arch of Renewal."

"Days? How many? I... I didn't agree to any of this..." she had started to dry wash her hands subconsciously.

"I know" he said, placing a very warm hand on her shoulder to calm her down. "Your children will be sleeping, remember that a day is but an hour. You won't be missed much. And I really want to make sure they do have a mom to return to them. Mossbrook is a de-salting town. Their main function is to produce fresh water and salt. Everyone in Estuarius knows how to fight and how to defend themselves but one thing is to know it and one other to experience it. The Protectors from the Capital are used to raids. I owe it to the world and to your children to wait for them."

"Yes, yes" she was feeling defeated. Every time she thought they were done with the adventure, one more delay seemed to surge out of nowhere "What are we to do while we wait?"

Gary perked up at the question, he had been expecting more resistance from his charge "well, like I said, everyone knows how to defend themselves and it seems that we'll be encountering some difficulty on the road. We do have a retired Protector teaching here so may as well get you as prepared as possible."

"Prepared how?" *he better be talking about putting provisions and transportation together, and how to hide under a rock.*

"Let's go to the Bushcraft Academy and see what you can do" Gary started walking purposefully once more.

"Oh, ok" *well that sounds like boy scout school.* Eliane had to do a little jog to catch up to Gary and promptly fell into step with him.

They arrived at a big field surrounded by trees. She noticed that no tubes of fresh water were coming to this part of the town. It was as if they had stepped out of the outer limits, but she could still see buildings far to each side before they made it to the center of the field. The sun was bright, reflecting off the brook running through the trees, the big mossy rocks that bordered the small stream looked perfect for sitting and dipping your feet in the cool water. On the left side of the field, a large area was clear of trees and, instead, had plenty of benches for sitting. They were all stacked one over the other, like bleachers at a stadium. But no stadium would have painted the benches in the same tones of the nature surrounding it, making them a harmonious part of the view.

"What is this place? It's beautiful" Eliane asked in awe, looking around, trying to take all the scenery in.

Gary chuckled before answering "This is where the Bushcraft Academy teaches and practices weaponry and outdoor survival skills. Anyone is welcome to come, students, villagers, and visitors alike. Its doors are always open."

"Sounds… fun" she said a bit apprehensively.

"Glad you see it that way" They were walking towards the trees, the sound of the brook music to their ears.

"Where is everyone then?" Eliane always loved the sound of water. She hoped they would make it all the way to the stream.

"It's vacation time so school is on break. You will only see patrollers practicing, the occasional townsperson, and of course, the Malauri."

"Malauri?" They were definitely going in the direction of the water. Maybe she could suggest to Gary they have a picnic there.

"I believe you call them educators. Malauri Faelan, like most Malauris in the academies, lives here."

"Is that my cue to show up?" said a melodic voice from the trees. Eliane's jump of surprise took all thoughts of the small stream right out of her head.

"Faelan! Yes, please, I would love to introduce you to someone" Gary's smile was so wide, it almost divided his face in two. The delight at meeting an old friend was clear in his voice.

"Well met Guider" the melodic voice was coming from the most beautiful woman Eliane had ever seen. Her brown eyes were the perfect shade to go with her caramel skin. She had a small, curved scar from her temple to her forehead, dividing her eyebrow in two sections. Eliane's breath caught. She thought she would never have said that someone was perfect, that was until today, at least.

"Well met Malauri. This is Eliane, her blood will sing in the Renewal" Gary introduced them.

Faelan looked at Eliane and with a slight inclination of her head she said "Hello Luimena Eliane".

"H-hi" Eliane greeted, feeling heat rising to her face. She wasn't sure whether or not it was from embarrassment at the catch in her voice.

Faelan was taller than most of the people Eliane had seen in town. She had long teal hair that cascaded in curls all over her shoulders. Her cream outfit resembled both overalls and a dress at the same time.

"What can I do for the two of you, Guider?" Faelan seemed to have dismissed Eliane in favor of her dark companion.

"I assume you have heard about the Dust Raiders?" After Faelan's quick nod, he continued "I thought we could make sure Eliane here can hold her own in a raid."

"What's your weapon of choice?" This prospect seemed to have made Eliane interesting again as Faelan turned to regard her with an air of excitement.

"Weapon of choice..." Eliane gave an awkward laugh – *I'm a middle-aged mom that works at a desk!* – "I, I don't have one."

Faelan's smile grew bigger, and she seemed to now be dancing on the ball of her feet "are you proficient in many weapons, then?"

Eliane was sure her face was going to melt out of sheer embarrassed blushing "the opposite" she managed to whisper hoarsely.

Faelan's excitement disappeared as quickly as it had appeared. She was all business again "let's see what type suits you better then" and without a glance back, she started walking toward what looked like a big shed.

Eliane stole a glance at Gary who nodded encouragingly towards Faelan "ermm, bye, I guess."

"Best of luck, Eliane" Gary seemed to be containing a laugh. What could be so funny, it was anybody's guess.

Eliane was out of breath – *of course I'm out of breath in front of her!* – by the time she caught up with Faelan who had been walking at the briskest of paces.

They entered a small building filled with weaponry. The walls were covered from top to bottom, Eliane could see several sticks, other sticks with metal ends, pointy ends, axe ends. She could see coils of rope of different thickness, swords in all shapes, skinny swords, long swords, short swords, broadswords, pointy swords, curved swords. There were axes, hatches, moon axes, double axes, poleaxes, throwing knives, and throwing stars, were those daggers? There were also bows, longbows, crossbows, and so many other things that she didn't have a name for. Everything looked organized, clean, and well maintained.

Faelan walked towards the section that was mostly comprised of swords and grabbed one that was sheathed in its scabbard and carefully pulled it out. It had a single-edged blade and looked very similar to the katanas of Earth.

"Have you seen one of these before?" she asked while moving the sword and letting the blade catch the light.

"I have seen similar, yes" – Eliane had seen them in movies and videogames.

"Oh good, so you are familiar with how they work?" Eliane thought she detected a hint of hope in her teacher's voice.

"I know this one! I heard the advice 'just stick them with the pointy end'" she said hopefully.

The look on Faelan's face was all Eliane needed to know that she had failed that particular test – *that shows me for taking sword lessons from TV.*

"I mean… you *can* 'stick them with the pointy end' but you would only do that in the stomach or the throat. You wouldn't want to stab a place with too much muscle or bone. This style is for slashing only" If there was hope before, there was no hint of it now. Faelan continued stiffly "the children know this, but you are not one of us" Eliane felt her back grow stiff. She knew this was not said with malice but rather as a fact, but she couldn't help feeling a sting at the words. "Here" the instructor continued, "grab it with two hands like this and make a motion like this" she explained while demonstrating with fluid movements.

Eliane held it with sweaty palms and a slight tremor. It was much heavier than she thought it would be.

"Your arms need to be higher" Faelan instructed adjusting Eliane's arms with short and sure movements "your elbow needs to be here, no, firmer, let it flow, relax your shoulders" As Faelan spoke, she kept one hand on Eliane's back while the student did her best to follow the instructions and to repeat the motions over and over again.

Within minutes, Eliane was sweating, her arms were trembling, and her shoulders felt as if on fire. She refused to give up and continued the exercises with stubborn ferocity.

"There's no point, this seems to be too heavy for you and we do not have the time to develop the necessary muscles.

How about a short sword?" Faelan slid the single-bladed sword back into its scabbard and placed it into its original place. "This one has a pointy end to stick it into someone" Faelan smiled and presented Eliane with a short sword she took from the wall. It wasn't bigger than a kitchen knife, but it was definitely pointy and with 2 edges. The blade was about a palm wide in its widest part. The handle was wrapped in a well-worn purplish leather that was soft to the touch, yet allowed Eliane to keep a firm grasp.

Faelan had Eliane go through a series of exercises with the blade. She soon realized that, even though this blade was the proper weight for Eliane, her pupil was too inexperienced for the close combat necessary for this type of weapon.

After putting the short sword away, the Malauri grabbed a bow with a quiver full of wooden arrows. They had gorgeous blue and violet fletching from some of the birds that Eliane had seen on her walk to the town. The bow was topped with one single blue feather. Faelan showed her an old target on a tree at the edge of the forested area and, with the most fluid of movements, took an arrow from the quiver at her back, notched it on the bow, and let it fly, hitting true, of course.

Silently, Faelan gave her both the bow and the quiver. Eliane threaded her arm and head through the loop so the quiver could rest comfortably on her back. She grabbed the bow, and after making a few attempts of reaching over her shoulder to get an arrow, she held the bow between her knees and with one hand she held the bottom of the quiver steady and with the other one she pulled the arrow. She notched it in place.

"You are holding the bow upside down; the feathered part goes upwards" the Malauri commented.

Red faced, Eliane flipped the bow and, once more, notched the arrow, then she pulled as far back as she could and let it go, it flew in a lazy arch and landed about a third of the way to the target.

"You need to make sure the bowstring is pulled back as far as it can go. You barely pulled it." Faelan remarked.

"Oh" Eliane tried one more time and pulled as far as her arm would go, trembling with exertion she asked, "like this?"

"That's not even halfway!" Eliane let go of the arrow in defeat and this time it made it just a couple of steps further than her first arrow.

While Faelan went to retrieve her own arrow, Eliane picked up hers, dusted them off, and put them back in the quiver. She handed everything back to her instructor who, silently, went back into the storage building to put everything away. The Malauri decided to have a better look at what Eliane's body could do. Outside in the fresh air, she put her through a series of exercises.

After what seemed an eternity, but it must have been less than an hour, they took a break. "I am afraid I do not know how to say this without offending you, Luimena" They were walking towards the brook. Faelan, looking straight ahead, back stiff, trying not to glance at her student. Eliane wasn't sure how to respond to that. She was just too thirsty and tired to think of anything else, so she just focused on the brook and kept on walking towards it – *eyes on the prize, eyes on the prize!*

They walked in silence and in silence they made it to the stream, dipped their hands in the cold water and washed their faces and hands while also taking big gulps on the welcoming liquid. Once they had drunk all they needed and picked the perfect rock, they sat and leisurely played in the water with their bared feet.

"Just say it how you see it" at first, Eliane thought the other woman had not heard her but after a few minutes of looking in the distance, she broke the silence.

"We are a peaceful people. We only had one big… horrific… war in our history." Faelan shuddered, as if the very mention of the conflict disturbed her. "Nobody alive today knows a grandchild of the fighters but we all know the cost and we all learned how to fight. We start training from the moment we take our first steps. We all have at least a basic knowledge of weapons. We believe in active bodies and keep our bodies fit. All of us. All. Not everyone dedicates their life to the physical. Some are scholars, some scientists, some engineers, some artists, some farmers. Regardless of our field of interest, we all know how to survive. We can survive in the wilderness alone without fear. We all know how to defend ourselves and our loved ones. You are said to come from us, but you have forgotten how your body works, how your body moves. You are unfit, unable to do a strenuous activity while keeping your breath even. I despair to think of your survival were you to find yourself apart from the Guider on your way to the Renewal."

They were quiet for a little while, one woman digesting what was said and the other one giving space. Eliane had her head turned to the sky, looking at the clouds lazily passing through the blue expanse – *what am I doing here? Why can't it be my friend that trains for a possible apocalyptic world here or my son's martial arts teacher?* – the sound of a little splash from a fish broke her reverie "You didn't offend me, you just told me the truth and for that, I thank you" Eliane saw a pair of perfect golden shoulders visibly relax before she continued "I cannot change how incredibly out of shape I am but I could try a few more weapons? Something that requires less abilities? And also, I am not that useless on the outside! Gary taught me a bit about herbs and what fruits to eat... and back home I was the one that started the campfires when we went camping. I bet I would survive at least two days. You and your super fit friends wouldn't need two whole days to find an out-of-shape human, would you?"

Eliane was delighted to see that her little quip had brought a lopsided smile to her instructor's face "no, we wouldn't need two whole days... Ok!" she rose and dusted off her outfit, ready for the challenge "we will find something we can do but first..." Faelan turned to look at Eliane and with a wide smile she declared "food!" as if Eliane needed more reasons to like her.

This was Eliane's first sit-down meal away from Earth. They were sitting at what she would have called a 'teacher's lounge', except it looked like a chick café in a little garden with metal tables and comfortable chairs that seemed to mold to her body. "Aren't they amazing? The cushions are made of hydrogel and magicked, so the water does not evaporate. It was designed by one of our science students. They are becoming quite popular everywhere!" Faelan was speaking very fast, obviously excited and proud of the accomplishment. Eliane was fighting the urge to reach for an errand lock of teal hair and tuck it behind her ear. Instead, she opted to match the other woman's energy.

"Yes! They are comfortable and quite beautiful. This shade of blue just goes so well with everything else here."

"It certainly does! We haven't yet been able to make them a different colour, but there's testing done for it. Oh, hi!" She greeted a rather large man that was now standing next to them with a content smile.

"Well met Malauri, Nere" he said with an inclination of his bald head "today's dinner is based on beans and vegetables. Are you looking for hot dishes or cold?"

"I'm afraid that I have been rather harsh with Luimena Eliane today, Food Bringer. She will need the sustenance of hot dishes. Would that be to your liking?" she turned to ask her pupil.

"Yes! Although, I wouldn't mind trying something cold too… to be honest, I have only foraged herbs and fruits on our way here."

"We simply can't have that!" said the man with mock horror "We cannot have the Luimena thinking that Estuarius is all uncooked food. I will speak with the Mestandil and give you an assortment of hot and cold to give you sustenance and pleasure. I will be back!" and with a happy step he disappeared through a wooden door set on the vine covered wall.

Watching him retreat, Eliane asked her companion "Could you explain something to me?" After a nod from the other woman, she continued "I'm supposed to be able to understand all the words but there are things that I don't understand.

After he called you Malauri, which I know means 'educator', he called me something and then he called me Luimena and then he spoke of a Mestandil. What do they all mean?"

"Yes, those are titles you get from learning at the Academy. I was a Nere. I am now a Malauri, I teach Neres, any person that is studying something is a Nere. The art of taking ingredients to make a dish, to prepare food is performed by the Mestandil."

"And speaking of art" interrupted the Food Bringer "here you are!" He placed a small bowl, more like a teacup without a handle, in front of each woman. The bowl had a greenish clear broth with a small red ball floating in the middle of it. In the center of the table, he placed a small wooden board with what looked like cheeses, dry fruits, nuts, and something that looked like asparagus. "I'll leave a board of colds for you to share, and I'll keep bringing small individual hots. Oh! Before I forget" he gave each woman a glass of water and placed warm wet towels on the side "May your meal comfort and nourish you" and with a bow, he left them to eat.

"Thank you very much Food Bringer" they both said with a smile. Eliane was happy, the soup was giving out the most magnificent smell. She could feel her mouth watering. She wrapped her hands around the bowl, taking a moment to feel the warmth before bringing the little bowl to her face. She inhaled deeply the rich and savory essence and brought it slowly to her lips, mindful of burning herself. She was expecting a mild chicken broth taste. Instead, she found a hearty and comforting savor reminiscent of earthy, wholesome warmth. It exuded a delicate blend of subtle umami notes, contributing to a depth of flavor that was simultaneously robust and mellow.

Faelan was studying her reaction "good, eh?" When Eliane nodded, she suggested she bit into the red gel. The surprise must have been very obvious in Eliane's face because Faelan busted out laughing "I love the mix too" she said still chuckling.

The gel let out a spicy, warm, and aromatic liquid that was both sweet and fiery, leaving a pleasant, tingling sensation on the tongue. Mixed in with the broth, it was like drinking a cozy warmth, reminiscent of the familiar, comforting taste of cinnamon, creating a pleasant and lingering sensation that suddenly made her ache for her home.

"Oh, what's wrong? Is it too spicy?" Faelan actually sounded worried.

"I... I miss my kids. I have been away from them before, but we still talked every day" she said, trying to keep tears from forming in her eyes "I'm completely disconnected from them. I know they are home, sleeping but they are just so far and out of reach" she sighed.

"Is there something you can do about that at this very moment?" She asked while biting into one of the green vegetables with a satisfying crunch.

"No" Eliane answered, wondering where the conversation was going.

"Then feel your feelings but don't let them stop you from living in the moment" Faelan said kindly.

"You are right..." with a smile she added "my oldest would love this food."

"Really? He likes hot food?" They talked and talked while

they ate, the soup was replaced by what looked like beans on a round chip, which was replaced by a vegetable stew that they ate using pieces of a warm flat bread as utensils. After they were done eating all their food, they got a delightful frozen dessert that was smooth and rich. The experience ended with an orange-coloured infusion that was supposed to aid them with their digestion.

As they sipped their floral tea, Eliane thanked Faelan for the chat as it had made missing her children more bearable. "Now let's go back to the academy so you can show me how you can light fires and see if there's anything Guider missed when teaching you about herbs."

The two women walked the training fields and into its forest where Faelan was pleased to see Eliane's knowledge of fruits and herbs in action. It was very basic, true, but it was enough to keep her well fed and away from anything that could make her sick. She would still have to teach her the medicinal herbs and how to find water when she could not see or hear a water source. About an hour later, they were back to the open field where Eliane successfully started a small fire with the twigs and bark they had collected. She used a flint stone necklace her husband had given her once because she had named herself the official fire maker during one of their camping trips.

While Eliane was starting the fire, Faelan had been setting up targets at various distances. She was now walking towards her with a crossbow resting on her shoulder.

"That is good fire Luimena" she congratulated before explaining "This is what those who can't stand or walk use for defense" the Malauri said while showing the wooden artifact to her student. "You put the string here, you tense it with this little crank" her fingers were dexterous, her movements precise "and then the bolt goes right here, like this" she showed. She then lifted the crossbow to her shoulder "brace the base against your shoulder like this. Aim using the end of the bolt, and release" the projectile left the crossbow with a little twang, and it flew true to the center of the closest target. "I think this one could be good for you."

As soon as Eliane grabbed it, she knew she was going to disappoint her instructor. The crossbow was long and heavy which made it hard for her to keep level with the ground. She put it aside while gathering the untouched wood into a neat pile on the ground. She was being very conscious of the curious eyes that waited patiently. Eliane then went belly to ground, she propped herself on her elbows, and rested the weapon on the pile she had made. She adjusted herself, aimed, and let go. It was not a perfect hit, but it was close enough to the center of the target to not matter.

"I'm glad to see you can use a crossbow, but you won't be able to set all this up when running from Dust Raiders. It's good, though. Not everything is lost. Let's see how you do with further targets."

They continued practicing until the light of day started turning gray "That is it for today, tomorrow we will try something a bit different, and we will continue your education on herbs."

Beaming, Eliane responded "the day just got better since our lunch; now if you could just point to a place where I could get clean… I'm afraid that 2 days of walking plus another one of physical exertion has made me rather musky. I mean I can actually taste my smell."

With the most melodic laugh Eliane had ever heard, the other woman responded "let us put all this away and clear the fire. I know the perfect place that will clean both our bodies and our spirits."

Faelan took her to the Academy baths. The building's lobby resembled a big waiting area with sofas. The door at the other end brought them to the change rooms where they took off their dirty clothes. Faelan tossed hers down a chute on the wall. When she noticed Eliane looking curiously, she explained "here at the institute we can choose to use the same garments. It makes it easier: you drop off your old dirty clothes here, it goes to the communal laundry room, and then grab clean ones after we are clean. If you have your own, you can store them over there" she pointed at what looked like lockers made of wood "and retrieve them once you are clean." Eliane left her dirty Earth clothes there – *I should burn these instead!*

They headed to a door framed by a shelf filled with cushions, they each grabbed one, and opened the door to a steam room. Eliane could barely see because of the steam, and she immediately started to sweat from every single pore. They sat on a bench, using the toweled cushions they brought in. Elaine opened her mouth to speak but the hot steam rushed in, making her cough so she decided to just lean her head onto the wall and breathed slowly in and out, in and out, her eyes closed, feeling the sweat running down her face. Enjoying the feeling of muscles relaxing, Eliane was starting to wonder how long they should stay there as her lungs were starting to feel uncomfortable, when Faelan touched her shoulder and indicated for her to follow. They exited the steam room onto another room that had what looked like four barrels in the center of it. They had small white rocks and big wooden ladles, the room smelled of salt and wood. Seeing her confusion, Faelan explained "that is salt from when we de-salt the ocean water to make it drinkable. We use it like this." She reached for a ladle and scooped a handful of very coarse salt and poured it on her hand, from there, she started rubbing her body with the salt.

Eliane exclaimed "oh! A salt scrub!" And proceeded to rub her whole body with it, including the armpits when she saw her mentor doing so. She scrubbed until she felt raw. They walked to the side of the room and stood over the grates. Right above them there were barrels filled with water, they pulled on the rope attached to the barrels and they spilled warm water over them. They repeated this several times until they felt that the salt had all been washed away.

They exited the room to another that had what seemed like a square pool taking almost the entirety of the space. Faelan dove into it and exited on the other side in just one breath "I like just a very quick dive, it's the best way to get this part over with!" Eliane followed suit and with the iciest of shocks, she understood why the need of getting it over with. The water could have come from a freezer for all she knew. It was a wonder it had not frozen solid already "that was unpleasant!" Faelan just laughed and exited the room to another one with only two pools. You could see steam rising out of the big one. "The small one is there in case you want to have a flower scent, just go in and out and you are done, it's not freezing cold, do not worry. Let's go to rest in the hot water, it will be pleasant."

They sat in comfort on the built-in bench that was all around the perimeter of the hot pool, careless of their nudity, enjoying the healing properties of the hot water.

"How does the water stay clean?" Eliane asked as she could not smell the chemical scent she associated with hot tubs and pools.

"You can only come here after cleaning your body in the other three stations, that helps cut down any grime. However, water is always moving, there is a constant stream of water coming in and water leaving. The water that leaves goes directly to the 'Used Water Treatment Facility', once clean, it goes back into the cycle of clean water. A ten-day before you arrived, the Dust Raiders attacked one of the pipes that transport water to the main city. We were all surprised. We are thankful the damage did not disrupt the flow."

"All this talk of Dust Raiders. Who are they?" Eliane asked.

"Dust Raiders are believed to be humans that found themselves on this side of the belt," she explained, "grown bitter by their inability to adapt to this world while being convinced that everything would be better if we just adopt the Earth's technologies."

"How very colonial of them..." Eliane commented under her breath with sadness.

"What has made the Dust Raiders more worrisome lately, is that they seem to have Tech Golems" she continued, unaware of Eliane's words "We are not sure how they can make them as they do not have any magic, but there are animations made with pieces of technology that have drifted into our world."

"Tech Golems… That really sounds like it needs magic. They wouldn't be robots; I don't think there would be enough parts coming through and all the right people to make a working robot in Estuarius."

"We really have no idea what or how, but they disrupt all our magic and if we get too close, we get dizzy and disoriented."

They decided to change the subject. Faelan had so many questions about what electricity really was and Eliane did her best to answer. Once they both felt that their muscles were nice and relaxed, they got out of the hot bath and Eliane came face to face with Gary.

"Was the water too hot? Your face is very red" he asked as Eliane was just standing there, completely naked, wondering why Gary was in their bathing room.

"Her face does that a lot, you should have seen her when we undressed." Interjected Faelan "It may be how humans react when they get cold quickly. Although I don't remember it being that red after the cold rinse."

"Hi Gary, the change room is that way" said Eliane, trying to change the subject. Her embarrassment was being chased down by her irritation.

"Oh, I came for you" he said, extending them both a towel "I'm glad I found you, I wanted to show you to your sleeping quarters. I also brought you shoes" he smiled and gave her a pair of green shoes; they looked more like socks with a sole, but she wasn't about to complain. The last thing she wanted was to put her dirty socks back on.

"Thank you, I'll be right back!" She accepted the offer and quickly went to the change rooms. Faelan found her standing in front of the place where all the clean clothes were.

"Need some help?"

"Yes, sorry, I must look stupid, but I do not know what to grab or how I would know whether it fits me."

"No need to call down yourself. I saw how many things you removed; I would be confused as well. Oh, are you cold again?" Eliane had turned bright red at the thought of Faelan watching her get undressed.

"No, no, it's all good" she said dismissively, urging the other woman to continue.

"These undergarments would fit you" she said, giving her a pair of very soft shorts like boxers "all the corinquas are the same size and you just wrap them around your body."

"Thank you, you are a great Malauri!" She said sincerely. The other woman replied with a smile that made Eliane's heart skip a beat until she remembered that they were both still naked, so she turned around quickly to avoid any more questions about her red face.

She first put on the shorts which she assumed worked as underwear. The second piece – *corinqua?* – seemed to be a pair of baggy pants with small straps at the bottom of the legs, that she could just tie around her ankles. Then from the top front of the pants, a square of fabric with two long wide straps attached to it – *ooooh they are overalls!* – she put the garment on but was unsure how to tie them "ehm, Faelan, how do I tie these?" she asked, holding the top part.

"Yes, of course" she grabbed the fabric from Eliane and

proceeded to explain "first you want it to cover your front, you don't want the sun burning your breasts" she held the square up to the taller woman's chest, "we then cross these behind you, make sure they do not bend or twist as that would make it uncomfortable and can dig on your back" she said making an X on her back, "then bring them to the front and up again" she made a sort of binding on Eliane's chest "to avoid them bouncing too much and causing you pain. Then under the arms and over your shoulders for support, now you just tie around your waist as much or as little as you'd like. I personally do not like having too much of a tail hanging to avoid tripping on it while climbing on things."

"Thank you!" Eliane found the corinqua to be very soft and comfortable "would we need re-tying during exercise?"

"No, everything stays in place" she answered with a smile.

Eliane gave a couple of hops just to make sure everything was in place and smiling said "This place really *is* magic!"

They were both sharing a laugh when they met Gary outside of the bathing building where they said their goodbyes.

Guider and Luimena left the academy and started walking towards a not too far building. The water pipes above reflecting the collected sunlight, the light looked warm and inviting, setting the perfect mood for an evening stroll.

Eliane noticed how Gary seemed to disappear when passing through darkened places. His dark clothes and skin made him blend with his surroundings. A loud growl of her stomach made her forget the disappearing illusion and Gary steered them towards a person standing at the side of one of the many parks. They had a metal box in front of them.

To Eliane's delight, the metal box was actually a cover to keep bean pies hot. They each grabbed one and ate it on a park bench. Once satisfied, Guider and human continued their walk to the nearby building. It was four stories high and had a lovely garden full of blue, violet, and white flowers on the front.

"Here we are" Gary exclaimed once they made it to the building's garden. "This is one of the sleeping buildings of the academy, they are for the Neris that do not have a house of their own. It is also used for those visiting the town. Let me show you to your quarters."

They entered the squat building and they found Eliane's room on the first floor. It was just like she would expect in a dorm: a small room with a single bed and a table with a chair.

Gary gave her bread baked with nuts. It was packed into a neat piece of folded fabric "so you can break your fast come the morning", and he left her with the promise of getting her at first light. She stripped down to her shorts, climbed into bed and covered herself up the neck with the warm and heavy blankets. She drifted to dreamland wondering how she would ever fall asleep with so many things to think of.

# | 4 |

# Training, So Much Training...

The following morning after Gary dropped off Eliane at the training grounds, Faelan asked her how her night had been. Not caring whether that was one of those questions people ask not really expecting a real answer, Eliane replied "I slept great but now everything hurts. I didn't know I had so many muscles in my body! I almost asked Gary to carry me here. I am honestly miserable!"

Faelan just stared at her for a few minutes in silence, then motioned her pupil to follow her to the comfort of the trees. Once there, Faelan motioned Eliane to sit on the floor, which she did with the grace of a straight and rusty rod. "Wait for me here and untie your corinqua, I need to get something first" said the Malauri before she left her. Eliane was not about to argue, she loosened up the knots of her outfit and rested her head on the tree behind her. She closed her eyes, content to listen to the flow of the brook while she waited.

A little while later, Faelan arrived and kneeled next to Eliane "This balm will take the pain and the stiffness away from your sore muscles. May I rub it on you?"

"Oh yes, please!" Faelan started on her shoulder and continued down her arms and even massaged her fingers. Then back up to the shoulders, neck area, face, down the back. Eliane felt her face going red while the other woman massaged the balm on her buttocks. The more she thought of the pleasure of the touch, the redder her face would get. She didn't want her to stop because it was really helping the soreness. Every part that had been massaged had been left with a little tingly sensation – *it's like my muscles are happy!* – but she also did not want Faelan noticing her flushed face, so she decided to strike a conversation while enjoying the feelings. "I am enjoying my stay, but it feels odd not having my dog with me all the time. I have always lived with a dog, so I am used to always talking with someone even when I'm supposedly alone."

"What is a dog?" Asked Faelan while she dug her fingers on a particular stubborn knot.

"It's a type of animal. He lives with me" Eliane answered while thinking of her beloved companion. "My dog's name is Doggie, the kids named him, and he is very fluffy and smart."

"Oh, like Milda!" she said excitedly.

"What is a Milda?" Eliane asked interested – *could it be a cat?*

"Milda!" She stopped rubbing the balm and took what

looked like a large pompom out of her pocket and placed it on Eliane's lap. "That is Milda" and she continued her work.

Eliane took the pompon on the palm of her hand, and it unfurled into what looked like a green sugar glider "oh my goodness she is so cute!"

"*He*" Faelan emphasized "belonged to my sister but she died in a stupid accident, so he now lives with me."

"Oh, I am sorry about your sister."

"Thank you. I miss her. She was always the climber." Faelan had stopped massaging and now had a faraway look in her eyes, remembering. "One day she decided to climb the tallest tree, she had done it before, she loved doing it. So up she went but this time she said she was going to do it faster than the count of ten dozen. And she did it, she was almost a blur, not stopping to think, she just went up as fast as I've ever seen her climb. She was so happy when she made it, she had to do a silly victory dance." A sad smile touched Faelan's lips as she recalled her sister's antics. "She was never a good dancer, and when you are that high up a tree, full of the excitement of the race… she lost her footing, fell to the ground, broke her neck along the way. It was an instant death, nothing that could be fixed." The woman's smile was gone, replaced by sadness. Her stare fixed somewhere far away, seeing without seeing, her mind lost in the traumatic memory.

They were both quiet for a while, what can you respond to a story like that? So Eliane just reached and placed her hand on the Malauri's shoulder and gave her a gentle squeeze. Faelan seemed to come back from her memories, looked at her and gave her a sad smile "It has been two years" she said quietly. Eliane pulled her in for a hug and they hugged tightly until Milda chattered in protest. They shared a little awkward laugh while they both wiped unshed tears. Faelan continued massaging her student.

"Well, Milda is an adorable little guy!" The Luimena broke the silence, studying the pet. He was tiny, about 14 centimeters long if you didn't count his long furry tail. His fur was soft and light green with a blueish stripe running down his back from top of the head to the tip of his bushy tail. He was looking at Eliane with large, expressive golden eyes that seemed to look right inside her soul. Eliane could see a thin membrane of skin stretching from his wrists to his ankles. She was holding his little hands when Faelan spoke again.

"My sister loved his claws... she taught him to use them in battle" Faelan got a happy dreamy sort of look on her face while talking about her sister "She taught him to attack the enemy's eyes" she sounded full of pride for her sister's accomplishment.

"How?" Eliane was stunned by the prospect of a little furry animal that fit comfortably on her cupped hand being used in a fight.

"She tossed him at the enemy's face and Milda would claw them. Awesome little self defense companion" Faelan reached a scarred hand and delicately touched one of his round ears before bopping his little pink nose with affection. "Give him back before you travel back to your homestead. I find that rubbing his soft tummy brings comfort. And knowing that one more set of eyes are watching your back gives me peace. He loves to eat insects and fruits. You have to be careful and give him first taste of your own fruit because his sharp teeth may get you if he tries to steal a piece. He mostly sleeps during the day, and he will stop any and all crawlers from getting into your bed while sleeping outdoors. A better companion does not exist!"

Milda made a little sound of approval at the compliment and jumped to catch a flying bug that got too close to them. The two women shared a laugh watching him eat. Eliane found herself drawn to Faelan and her melodious mirth.

Faelan stood up, wiped off her hands on her pants, declared "Today we are trying a few new things!" And started walking towards the weapons' shed without a backwards glance.

Eliane watched the woman go. She held Milda up to her face and asked him "does she always just leave and expects to be followed?" Milda just sat on her hands, cleaning his whiskers, "you are right, we have to do it!" She put Milda in the deep square pocket on her right leg where he immediately curled up to sleep the day away. With a smile, Eliane shook her head and got up, dusted her hands off and went after her teacher while tying up her corinqua.

Faelan came out of the shed right before Eliane was getting there. The Malauri had a long stick in one hand, a small box in the other, and a belt around her waist – *am I going to learn to hit people with a belt? Hahaha*

"Here, hold this" she instructed, giving Eliane the box. She held the stick with both hands "don't let that box drop and tighten your core" Eliane did as instructed but she was getting nervous about it. With her usual speed, Faelan swung the stick towards her student's left arm. With a loud screech, Eliane swung her left leg back while bringing the box up and to the left to meet the weapon. The shock of the stick hitting the box traveled up her arms.

"What the Hell?!" Eliane shouted angrily, still holding onto the box, looking at her smiling instructor.

"Hey, your reflexes work!" she said clearly thrilled.

"Oh really?!" The student asked, full of venom.

"Yes, really" the Malauri replied, completely missing the sarcasm in Eliane's voice. "That means there's hope! Ok, ok, you can put the box down, let me teach you a few things with the quarterstaff."

"Are you going to beat me some more first?" She was starting to calm down – *quarterstaff, not a stick, I knew that* – She put the box down slowly, not taking her eyes off of the other woman.

"Good! Good! Always keep an eye on the danger" it was impossible to remain mad when your instructor was beaming so happily at you.

"Fine, give me the stick" She held out her hand.

"Quarterst.." Faelan started to say when Eliane interrupted with finality "Stick."

The Malauri laughed loudly and handed her the quarterstaff and they proceeded to do exercises for half the morning.

After putting the big stick away, they went to the brook for a break. Faelan took out a piece of fabric and unfolded it over her lap, revealing some sticky looking pieces of something that looked like fruit slices "my favorite dry fruits covered in honey, want some?" Eliane helped herself and was really glad she did as it was the perfect mid morning treat. She could really tell why it was the other woman's favorite.

"I wasn't horrid, was I?" Eliane asked between bites.

"No, you were not. But you did trip a lot" Faelan answered and then started to giggle "you looked a bit like you drank too many fermented juices!"

Eliane looked at her incredulously – *I did not look drunk, it's easy to trip with a long stick hahahaha 'trip with a long stick!'*

Faelan took her student's giggles as agreement "we cannot have you tripping on your weapon out there. We'll try the whip when we are done here."

As soon as they downed the last piece of the candied fruit, Faelan stood up, rested her hand on the intricately etched buckle, and with a quick and skilled motion, she effortlessly uncoiled a whip. She smiled at Eliane's stunned face and said, "this is my favorite accessory of all times" and with a short wrist movement, she took down a leaf from the closest tree. The crack of the whip resounded, echoing its dual nature as both an accessory and a weapon.

"I had no idea that was a whip!" Eliane said excitedly.

"I know!" her instructor replied with a big smile "I had it made so the handle would seamlessly integrate into the buckle. I don't like having it dangling on the side."

Faelan offered the handle to Eliane, she could tell that the whip was made of high-quality leather, providing a smooth and polished appearance while ensuring resilience "it's beautiful!"

"And deadly" added Faelan.

"Beautiful and deadly, better than silent and deadly" said Eliane with a smile.

Faelan looked at her student with horror "Luimena! It's

better to be silent than beautiful, how else do you expect to sneak upon your enemy?!"

"It… it was a joke." She replied in an embarrassed whisper.

"I really do not understand Earth humour. Let's see how you do with this weapon."

After an hour of trying different things, Faelan declared "you will only be allowed to touch a whip again when I want you to lose an eye, not before!" She extended her hand towards Eliane and the woman gave her back the whip. The seasoned instructor took the weapon and, in two fluid movements, it went back to being a belt. "Let's try this" she said after going through the box she had brought out of the shed earlier. In one hand, she had a sling, and in the other, a weighed down bag. Eliane tried twice to shoot the pebbles from the bag to the nearest targets but, like with the bow, she couldn't stretch the band far enough for it to be effective. Afterwards, they tried throwing knives, but Faelan's increasing frustration made them give up. Eliane could hit the targets just never point first.

"I guess it would only be a crossbow for you. I was really hoping for something you could also use on the move. No problem, we shall adapt. Here" she offered her student what looked like a diamond shaped leather piece with three larger hoops of the same material coming out of it.

"What is it?" Eliane asked her, taking the leather, it was soft and strong, the hoops seemed to be adjustable. She couldn't tell whether the blue hue was due to it being stained or it was naturally that colour.

"For the crossbow: Put your arms through the smaller hoops, you can open the one bigger like this" she said showing her how to slide the strap "and tie it around your waist. The crossbow gets attached to this part" she said pointing out a retractable piece that Eliane hadn't notic[ed] [be]fore "the crossbow will then remain in place, secured o[...] [...]tch. When you need to use the crossbow, [...] and the patch will let go of it, then [...] behind you to use it, and then toss it b[...] no need to detach it, you can pract[...] and I have a surprise for you."

Eliane was so focused on the ex[...] the crossbow holster that at first [...] words "What? A Surprise? What[...]

"You won't be alone with m[...] lan declared happily "One of th[...] tomorrow. They will be joini[...] groups."

Eliane was not sure how[...] thanked her teacher for t[...] where he had been resting [...] with her thoughts.

After a pleasant bath [...] "Hey Milda, ready to s[...] her furry friend. He w[...] occasionally reached up to p[...] some fruits for Milda so off they went to [...] when she first arrived at Mossbrook.

"Hello! Where have you left the good Guider?" the Shop Keeper recognized her as soon as she came in.

"It's just me and Milda here" she responded pointing at her furry companion "I've been told he is a big fan of fruits."



this pie with the vegetables he grew. You just wait and see; a little taste and you won't want to go back to Earth!"

Eliane thanked him and continued her walk, this time looking for the perfect place for 'people watching' like her grandmother used to call it. She chose a bench in a nearby park where she could watch the children playing and the people walking the streets. She placed the basket next to her and Milda jumped in, grabbed one of the fruits, and perche[d] himself on the back rest to enjoy his meal. Eliane chuck[led] wished him to enjoy himself and took out the pie "the Sho[...] she said to the furball around a mouthful "the Sho[...] was right, his beloved can really cook!"

Once Milda was done with his fruit, he cli[mbed] got in between the many vines that wer[...] the water pipes. There he proceeded [...] moths that were attracted to the ligh[...] done with her fruit and Milda h[...] the woman said, "let's go home[...] and sleep."

Back in her room, she[...] rest to Milda. She left [...] case he got hungry d[...] she saw a new fo[...] morning "I bet[...] sleeping, ok?[...] happy ch[...] place. [...] to h[...]

while ta[king] [...]

"And wait until you [...] Estuarius! My beloved always cares f[or] [...]

As promised, when Eliane made it to the training grounds, there were ten people there that she had never seen before. One had fiery red hair like out of a cartoon, others had it brown, black, blue, and even green. She wondered if the ebony woman dyed her hair white or if it was natural – *she could be a drow!* – Eliane was a bit intimidated by the group, they all looked intense and moved with the same feline quality that Malauri Faelan always displayed but that she hadn't seen in anyone else.

"Ah! Here is Luimena Eliane" her friend introduced her when she spotted her in the back, "Eliane, this is Malauri Arawn" she added, pointing to a burly man standing next to her. He was missing an ear and had an ugly scar that disappeared into his long strawberry blond hair. Everybody waved awkwardly while Faelan pretended not to notice. "Alright, now that the niceties are out of way, we will follow the same formula every day. We start with stretching and strength exercises, then each one of you will individually practice with your own weapons. Then we'll do obstacle courses, break for lunch. Once you are done eating, it's back here to work on your herb's knowledge, survival skills, and hand combat." She was looking at everyone as she spoke, making sure every single person was paying attention. Arawn at her side did the same. "At the end of the day we'll do a group exercise with different simulations of Dust Raiders ambushes and drills. Understood?"

"Yes, Malauri!" the group said in one voice. It was loud and unexpected; it made Eliane jump in surprise.

The day had gone exactly as Faelan had said it was going to go. At the beginning, the others acted awkwardly, unsure on how to behave around Eliane. By the end of the day, they had welcomed her as one of them.

She only remembered that the baths were not only communal but also unisex when they went in as a group. Eliane hesitated for a moment in front of the door to the change rooms – *meh! When in Rome...* – she went through the door, and she continued the conversation she was having with one of her new companions. Afterwards they all had dinner together. The following day was the same with only a small variation on the group exercise.

The fifth day since Eliane's arrival to Mossbrook, was the day of rest. It was a good thing that Gary had visited her the evening before and told her; otherwise, she would have gone to the training grounds as it was her routine now.

She spent the day exploring the city and its gardens, enjoying the music coming from different places. Her new group of friends found her playing with Milda at a park later that afternoon. They invited her over to a tavern for fermented drinks and foods to which she gladly accepted.

The tavern was a house that she had passed by many times. It had a sign with what looked like a mug of ale on it. They went inside and she was welcomed by exactly what you would expect of a pub on Earth. It was dark, smelled like beer, and had music playing in the background. There was a bar that had a multitude

of bottles on display behind it. And the bartender greeted everyone with a wide and genuine smile "I'll send Anaya with drinks and food, sit wherever you please!" he said as a way of welcome.

The group sat at the very first table where they could all fit. Anaya served them all what looked like beer as well as a couple of boards with cold foods and dips – *beer, charcuterie board, and dips, yes!* – Eliane took a tentative sip, and it was, indeed, beer. It was light and foamy and just what she had wished for. She grabbed a vegetable, dipped it into the creamiest sauce she could find on the table, and leaned back to enjoy herself. She took pleasure in the group's company. They were young, happy, and full of life. They always had stories and the most ridiculous of observations. She was really enjoying herself and sneaking some of the nuts to Milda when a fight broke out.

It was so fast and unexpected. It happened a few tables over, but it soon spilled out to the rest of the tavern. Eliane's companions immediately went into patroller mode and tried to control the situation. She knew she did not have the skill to participate so she simply backed away and hopped into the bar. From her vantage point, she saw one of the original fighters coming behind one of her friends. Without a single thought spared for her actions, she took off one of her shoes and threw it directly to the guy's head. It didn't do much damage, but it caused enough of a distraction for her friend to turn around and subdue him. Just as that was happening, Eliane saw the one who had started the fight lift a barrel over his head and walk towards Anaya, which prompted her to lose her leftover shoe. The broken nose, courtesy of her well aimed projectile, made him lose his grip on the barrel which felt right on his head, knocking him unconscious. Now that the main instigator was out cold, the kerfuffle came quickly to an end.

Eliane was elated, it was her very first bar fight! "I think you lost this!" one of her companions called out, throwing one of her shoes back, she had to duck to avoid the missile. Laughing, she jumped off the bar, retrieved it, and put it back on. "Have you seen the other one? She called out to him." This time Anaya answered "here! But it's wet. No! Stay there, the floor is full of broken glass!" she said to Eliane when she started walking towards her second shoe. So Eliane sat back down, Milda started chattering from her shoulder "oh! Yes, I could had thrown you but I rather you kept me safe here" It was a good thing that that seemed to mollify the pet, she was not about to start putting him in danger any time soon. With a content smile, she petted the furball and watched as people started to settle back down, some of them already drinking, as if nothing had happened.

That night she went to bed after a sobering bath, with a feeling of belonging that she hadn't experienced before in the strange world.

Two days after the events at the tavern, Gary knocked on Eliane's door as she was enjoying her breakfast. After she invited him in, he sat at the edge of her bed, looking content.

"I have brought something for you" he said, opening the package he had with him.

She took it from his too-warm callused hands. "What is it?" It looked like leather arm sleeves each with two metal inlays, one next to the other.

"I don't have a name for it yet, but it is for you" He answered while she studied one of the artifacts.

Eliane threaded her arm through it and rested it on her forearm. It had loops on it to make it tighter, which she did. She then proceeded to do the same with the other one. They were comfortable and didn't weigh much despite the metal inlays. "Are they vambraces?"

"Yes and no. They are more than vambraces as they are also a weapon."

"A weapon?! How can glorified arm sleeves be a weapon?" she asked, confused.

With a laugh, Gary got up from the bed and went to her. With deft fingers, he pulled one of the metal inlays loose and it immediately became a straight oval in his hands "you can detach this and toss it at someone. On impact it will send a pulse that will knock the person unconscious. It has the shape and weight of the sole of the shoes you threw in the bar fight."

"Are you serious?!" Eliane was laughing delightedly. "How?!"

"As soon as I heard of what you did, I knew exactly what your weapon of choice was: shoes. But we cannot have you walking barefoot around in battle, so I went to the blacksmith and with plenty of work and magic, we designed these. Here, feel it."

She grabbed the oval on her hand, and it was perfect, it looked rigid, but it was bendable, it was also cold and smooth to the touch.

"To put it back, just slap it onto the vambrace."

She did exactly that "oh wow! Like a snap bracelet" she was delighted "this is so cool!"

Gary was smiling. "You have two on each arm, that's four projectiles." He said, helping her to take the vambraces off. "Once you throw them, you lift your arm in the air. The discs are magicked to fly back to it and slap themselves into place" he explained.

Eliane's eyes were as big as saucers – *like Thor's mighty hammer!* – "oh my god".

"That's not all" he smiled – *how can it get better?* – "your vambraces also work as a shield. If someone, or something, tries to hit you, you can just lift your arm and it will stop the blow" – *Like Wonder Woman!* – "The arm plate will absorb the shock and throw it back out in a physical pulse, like a shock wave away from the holder."

Eliane didn't know what to say. She just stared at the Guider with her mouth hanging open.

"What do you think?" he finally asked.

"I... I can't believe it, they are perfect!" she rushed in for a hug. After an initial shock, Gary hugged her back, not noticing the happy tears in the woman's face.

"We should go meet the Malauris, we'll practice with these today" he said without breaking the hug. She let go and discreetly dried her face and led the way out of the room.

As they were walking, Eliane could still feel the warmth leftover from having hugged the Guider.

Hesitantly, she decided to ask Gary why his skin always felt hot to the touch like he is always running a fever.

"That's how my race is" he said as the sole explanation.

Eliane was surprised by the statement "You are not the same race as the people around us?"

Gary chuckled at her startled expression "not at all, I am part of a race that has been here for a very long time. We live for thousands of years. That is why there has only ever been two Guiders since we've had need of the Renewal, my father and me. My daughter would be the next one when I am no longer capable of Guiding a Luimena to Estuarius."

"Luimena, I know that is my title. Could you tell me the meaning?" – *he has a daughter?*

"It means 'of the blood'" he said with a smile. He always seemed to smile when explaining things to Eliane, like a proud teacher, or an amused parent. "You are the third Luimena to come to us and I think the next generation will have the fourth. I've seen too much Belt decay this time around. I think Earth is developing technology much faster than when we first started the Renewal. I am afraid it won't be another 106 Earth years but much sooner than that. We'll see, once I put it forward with the council."

*Council? Ok, one thing at a time* – "And… and why are those of your race Guiders?"

"Because we can stand the effects of technology better than any other race and we can innately open portals between our realities. Anybody or anything that passes between, does so by accident except for us. I have traveled many times to Earth, I can smell the magic in your lineage. Sometimes we will go just to feel if anyone has made it there by accident and rescue them from a gruesome fate. We have seen your world since it first came to be."

Eliane needed some time to digest this. How old was Gary? He didn't seem old at all. She would have put him in his early 30s back on Earth; although, he had mentioned that he met her great-grandmother.

They arrived for training and Gary stayed to see her test her new weapon. He threw a few things at her, which she deflected with the arm band. They also tested it with a quarterstaff, and it actually made it break "woah! That packs a bigger punch than I thought!" he exclaimed delightedly, holding only half of the original stick "let's try now with targets" He had her throw the bracelets to a target on his hand.

They kept practicing, especially getting one bracelet back while throwing the next one out. It took a while to get into the rhythm. Once they got it, they started practicing while moving. By the time they had to do group exercises, Eliane had it down fairly consistently.

After group practice, Malauri Faelan announced that since she seemed to have integrated so well with the patrol group, it had been decided that the group they have been training with will go with them to the Arch of Renewal.

* * *

After a long day of practice with Malauri Faelan and Malauri Arawn, the Renewal Group, as they had started calling themselves out of their Malauris' earshot, were all sitting by a fire on the training field near the brook. They were having fermented drinks, cold foods, and someone was playing a lute. A smaller group of them had been talking about one of their favourite subjects: the Luimena and her role in the Renewal. They had heard of the act, of course, it was part of their lore, and they were honoured that they were going to be present in such an important event that only occurred once every two and a half millennia. Of course, some of the things they talked about was how different Eliane was from what they had expected. She was just so... *normal* except she would say the oddest things whenever she got triggered.

"I think I'm starting to get some of the trigger words down." Said the shorter of the three companions. "Look at this" he instructed, then made sure that Eliane was still sitting close by. She was watching Milda eat a piece of fruit on her lap. He raised his voice to make sure it would reach the Luimena and said to the group "well of course, we would need to 'turn around' and face it." He said with an odd emphasis, then, in a whisper, he added "look at her!"

At once Eliane started saying – *is she singing?* – "turn around... every now and then I get a little bit lonely" she lowered her voice and continued saying something that they couldn't hear while bobbing her head as if dancing to a song only she could hear.

"Oh, she is missing her nucleus on Earth!" said the one with the fiery red hair, "don't use those words, they trigger homesickness!"

"Oh Blood!" swore the first one, "I hadn't made the connection! We are going to have to keep a diary of trigger words and their effects."

***

As usual, they all congregated in the empty field about an hour after first light. This time, the Malauris had a different training plan, today they were going out of town. "Today we are going to battle a patrol from Lakebog" explained Arawn.

Eliane leaned towards her companion and whispered, "What is Lakebog?"

"It's the closest city, come on! Let's get our things ready" he replied with a pat on her back and took off to a nearby building. Eliane followed the group behind, wondering how this was going to play out.

Amid excited talk, they collected their weapons and rations, and within the hour, they were lined up and ready to go.

They had a long, long walk in the forest. They started out a path but after a midday break, they walked only through the forest. They didn't break for the day until the sun had been hidden for at least 2 hours. That night, the Malauris reminded them to guard against 'dream eaters' as they were very common around those parts.

"Excuse me" Eliane did not like the sound of that "Did you just say, 'dream eaters'?"

"Yes" responded Malauri Arawn "that is exactly what I said... you do know them, right?" he asked in his usual rapid way of talking.

"First time I hear of them" she said, worried.

"They are night hunters that will invade your dreams. They trick your consciousness into staying with them" he explained. "We do not know what happens to the mind of those that fall pray to them, but we do know when they have succumbed because we can't wake them come morning.

Their bodies are left behind until they die of hunger. Those who have had close encounters talk of luring, pleasure, and abandon in their dreams."

Eliane definitely did not like the sound of that! "And how am I supposed to protect myself from those things?"

"Think of light, fall asleep dreaming of light, they do not like it. Stay away from the shadows in your dreams." He explained as if talking to a child.

"How? I'm unconscious in my dreams!" she asked, worried.

"You can't control your dream time?" Arawn seemed perplexed, as if Eliane was asking how to breathe.

"No." She answered with finality. She was annoyed at the tone of incredulity in his voice.

"Oh…" he seemed to remember that Eliane was from a different world and softened his tone "sleep in the center of the camp. Dream Eaters won't be able to reach the middle. Those stronger in the dreams will sleep on the edges. You will be safe. We will keep you safe" he reassured her.

She smiled at him and gave him a nod of thanks. She then turned around and went to look for a spot to sleep.

The following day, as they were getting ready, Eliane tried to get more information as to what to expect. The Malauris had mentioned that they were less than a day away from meeting the other group and she was getting anxious about the encounter. Fidgeting with the loops on one of her vambraces she asked one of her companions, the one with the freckles.

"We are going to simulate battle. We may walk into an ambush if we are not careful. We are not going to use any lethal force. All the edges and points of our weapons will get a shield to avoid hurting our companions. Oh, here comes Malauri Faelan to take care of our weapons."

"Greetings companions, may I please have your weapons?" Faelan said with a smile. She was always so formal when they were surrounded by the patrol. They still got to enjoy their private conversations at lunch time and sometimes after training. Eliane always matched the formality within the group, though, no point in doing otherwise.

"Armours on! We set out when you are ready!" shouted Malauri Arawn.

Eliane put on her cuisses and greaves, slid over her backplate and as she was putting on her breastplate, she commented to no one in particular "I'm glad that women's armours are not just a piece of leather that covers my breasts" it took her a couple of seconds before she realized that all activity around her had seized. She looked up only to find that her companions were looking at her in astonishment "what?" she asked them confused.

"Do Earth women not need protection of their vital organs?"

Eliane laughed "we do, we do..." and she continued adjusting herself. When they saw that she wasn't going to volunteer any more information, the rest of the group resumed their preparations.

Soon they were all on their way, the ease of the previous walk gone from their steps. They were now on alert, but they still talked about other exercises which helped put Eliane's mind at ease.

They made it to the base of a hill where the Malauris told them that their scouts had seen the others approaching.

They quickly hatched a plan where Eliane would act as a lookout on the top of the hill with the crossbow. She would signal when the other group made it past, and they would [shoot] from both sides. They were expecting to catch the other [grou]p unaware. Malauri Faelan had sent two runners to walk [b]ehind making noise while pretending to try at stealth. [Th]ey knew they had been spotted by the enemy's scouts.

They all nodded their understanding and left to take on their positions.

Eliane crawled to the top of the hill and set herself up with the crossbow resting in front of her, at the ready. Milda on top of her head. Vambraces on her arms. Faelan joined her so she could check on her friend's first battle drill "hey, how are you feeling?"

"Good, this is exciting!" she said with a nervous smile while the Malauri gave Milda a quick scratch on the head.

"I just wanted to ask you what was going to be your signal. Just so there are no confusions" she asked, all business again.

"Bird" she said firmly.

"Bird?"

"Yes"

"The word 'bird'" Faelan looked very confused which was rather amusing for Eliane.

"Yep, 'bird' is the word" Eliane was having a hard time keeping a straight face "I will also lose a bolt, in case someone cannot hear me."

Faelan went back to her position shaking her head but content with the plan. She did not notice Eliane chuckling quietly to herself while she resumed her surveillance.

* * *

The following days in Mossbrook were all the same. up, breakfast in her room with Milda, go to the Academdo some stretches, practice weapons, lunch, group exercises, then some socializing, and back to her room at the end of the day. Some exercises lasted well into the night. Training was so much different in the dark than it was in the daytime. At the end of her 14th day in Estuarius, the Protectors finally arrived at Mossbrook. The standby was finally over, tomorrow they were traveling to their final destination.

# | 5 |

# The Way to The Arch

Eliane had been thinking how different it is from reading about battles, to seeing them on TV, to actually living them, so many Dust Raiders were in pursuit, you could hear them coming, feel the explosions get closer and closer – *this is not the same, it's not the same, how am I going to continue? This is so scary oh God let me make it back to my kids!* – she made it to a crack on the mountain wall where Gary had been motioning everyone to go, she was the last one to make it in there – *always the last one, I'm so out of shape, this is SO NOT THE SAME!* – the Guider stood at the crack entrance, facing the enemy. With a guttural scream of defiance, he planted both his feet solidly in the ground while opening his arms wide, he screamed "You shall not pass!" Upon hearing these words Eliane stumbled, regained her feet and kept running with renewed energy – *well, maybe some things are the same* – an ear-splitting sound followed by a cloud of dust coming from behind her erased the smirk on her face as she fell forward, tumbling onto the rocky ground. A strange stillness fell on the group as they looked back at the cloud of dust, trying to understand what had just happened. As they watched, the sun seemed to hide behind a great shape, they could hear a sound like the canvas of a big tent flapping in the wind, one flap, two flaps, the sun was visible one more time, but the silence now felt oppressive. The strange stillness seemed to break as if by magic when Gary emerged from the dust cloud laughing "it feels so good to stretch!"

Eliane's fellow companions shared a relieved laugh with the Guider, hugging and patting each other's backs in celebration. Eliane stared at the wall of fallen rocks in front of her – *how did everything go so wrong?* – she was having a hard time reconciling the morning's easy walk with her current situation. They were all incredibly filthy from the rockslide and she could see blood on most of her friends. Movement between her breasts reminded her that she had shoved Milda there to protect him behind her breast plate. She now scooped him up "are you ok?" His fur was wet from her sweat, and he was just staring at her "we are safe now, you are safe now" in response, the little fur ball chattered and started to groom himself. She smiled, "you are a brave little guy" gave him a little kiss and placed him on her shoulder where he rubbed his face onto her neck before continuing with the grooming.

She did not notice Gary's stare on her, he studied her in silence as she followed the group away from the slide. It was the beginning of a detour that would add another three days to their trek.

They had left that morning in high spirits. The patrol that arrived a few hours earlier from the direction they were headed, didn't have any reports of Dust Raiders. Things looked good and there was no reason to worry. Familiar forest gave way to rocky terrain, as they walked parallel to the brook she was so fond of. Gary had told her that the brook was born of the river they needed to cross over. Faelan had mentioned that the river was treasonous and full of rapids as many other rivers converged with it high in the mountains that were on their left. The terrain and sheer drops making the water body full of rapids and strong currents. There was a beautiful bridge over the river, the only crossing point in miles. And it was at that very bridge where things started going terribly wrong.

The Protectors were leading the way, the Renewal Group bringing the rear. Gary and Faelan at each of Eliane's sides. The angry river louder than she imagined a river could sound, the white foam a protest against the rocks. The constant spray of water was forming a rainbow that softened the feeling of violence that the rapid waters evoked. When the people that were right in front of her were about to step onto the bridge, the bridge started to shake and then it collapsed. The group that had been on it did not stand a chance to make it to the other side even though they tried running when the movement started. It had caught them mid bridge, maybe if they had been close to reaching the other side... The churning river took away the pieces and with it the people that she had waited for all those days. In the blink of an eye, The Protectors were no more, swept away in the rubble. She did not have time to see if anyone was swimming to safety when something exploded next to her, pieces of dirt showering her "exploding kokos!" she heard someone yell "Take cover! Run towards the mountain!" she knew Faelan's voice anywhere, as usual, it was commanding and calm. Eliane looked around to see where they were going and followed as fast as she could, another explosion, more pieces of dirt raining down. She scooped Milda from her shoulder to protect him and he complied without chatter, trembling in her grasp.

They were running all out towards the cover of boulders and trees on the way to the mountain. She almost lost her footing while jumping the mossy rocks of her beloved stream, but Gary caught her and gave her support. "Hurry!" he implored, as if she needed any urging.

She heard a couple more explosions but all that mattered was to get to the cover, away from the explosions so they could then make it to the impossibly far mountain. When something was that big, it didn't matter how fast you ran, it didn't feel like you were getting any closer. "This way!" she heard someone shout ahead. She saw the group turn and she turned with them. She collapsed behind the big boulders as soon as she reached them.

Everyone was breathing hard, getting their weapons ready. Someone, she thought it could had been Malauri Arawn, casted a mirage to hide them from view. If they had a Tech Golem with them, it would pierce the illusion. Eliane wasted no time and set her crossbow – *what am I doing?* – she had been practicing but could she do it? A couple minutes later, the Dust Raiders arrived.

They looked like anyone would look on Earth, except they

were dirty, and their clothes had seen better days. Eliane and her group were hiding from them, praying the illusion would hold just as they were all holding their breaths. She knew she was not the only one aiming towards the enemy group.

"Regroup!" Eliane heard the word coming not far from where they had come, the Dust Raiders that were now among her group abandoned stealth and went back to their leader. She waited until she felt a hand on her shoulder, the familiar warmth telling her Gary was with her. She turned to look at him "We need to go to the mountains, quietly" he whispered. Milda creeped out of her clothes and rested on her shoulder. She reached up to pet him, unsure whether it was her or the furry friend who needed the reassurance.

They went quietly, hiding from boulder to boulder, behind trees, creeping here and there. They would freeze whenever they heard voices, then move again when the sound receded. It was nerve racking and a perfect recipe for anxiety, but she persevered. She had one goal and one goal only: to make it to the fissure on the mountain wall. Gary had pointed at it earlier and had let everyone tell the rest of them where they needed to go.

They made it to the edge of the forest, right to the natural line that divided forest from desolated rocky terrain that led to the fissure, nothing grew in the area, there were only rocks everywhere. They would be seen, there was no avoiding it. They started again in silence until a loud "there!" denounced their presence. They bolted, the opening was right there, they would make it. The explosions started again, this time making rock fragments rain all around them, but she made it. She made it through the crack and now she was sitting by a fire, watching the flames dance – *when did we get here?* – Milda jumped off her knee to catch a flying moth that was attracted to the flame "good catch Milda! Enjoy that juicy treat!"

"You are back with us" said Faelan gently next to her. "We were worried, you were walking like in a dream."

Eliane smiled weakly at her friend "I am sorry, that is my first near death experience."

"We all understand. Are you wounded? You do not seem wounded."

"I am alright, just tired. Do not worry about me, please."

"Here, eat this, a hot meal helps the invisible wounds."

Eliane took a bite from the wooden bowl, it was a delicious stew "this is definitely great medicine!"

Faelan left her to eat.

After finishing her food, Eliane just sat there, enjoying the fire, watching her companions laugh and Milda play. She was particularly invested in watching how the furball was stalking a bug when she thought she saw movement out of the corner of her eye. Against her better judgment, she grabbed the pet "come, I may need you" and went to investigate. At the edge of the fire, she hesitated – *don't I always scream at people in the books not to go investigating? Good thing this is real life and not a book!* – she went in the direction of the movement – *there it is again, is it an animal? No, it would have left already* – She was definitely not prepared for what she found. Sitting behind the bush was a little child, maybe 7 or 8 years old, not that much different from her own youngest kid. For a moment, neither of them moved, the child was just looking at her, eyes wide with fear. Eliane softened her face and visibly relaxed.

"Hi sweetie, you look a bit lonely there" she said softly. "Can Milda give you a bit of company?" she asked him, showing him the furball with slow movements so as to not spook him.

A small nod. "Milda, be nice and give company to our friend, ok?" Chatter from the little animal.

Eliane tossed him softly towards the child and Milda landed gently in front of him. "There he is, isn't he cute?"

Another nod. The child picked him up hesitantly.

"He is so soft and look! He likes you!" Eliane said when the little guy rubbed his face on the child's hand.

A small smile. Eyes on the furball.

"May I get closer?" Eliane asked.

A nod.

Eliane sat next to the child, in silence, they both watched Milda and chuckled softly. She didn't want to make any sudden movements.

"I am a little bit hungry; I have some candied fruits in my pocket. Is it ok if I take them out?"

A nod. He was now looking at her sideways, attentive.

She took out the treat that Faelan had given her earlier. She placed the fabric on the floor in front of her and unfolded it slowly, revealing the honey dipped strips of yellow fruit that her friend was so fond of. She took one and took a small bite "These are so tasty; would you like one?"

Another nod, this time it was faster, excited.

"Go ahead, take one" she instructed and like a little feral beast, he launched at the fruits and ate them all quickly. "We have more food by the fire. I will keep you warm and safe, I promise."

At first, he didn't move a muscle, then quietly said "are you a mom? My mom says to only trust other moms."

Eliane's heart just broke. How many times has she told her own kids that if they got lost to find the closest woman with kids to ask for help? "Yes, honey. I have two boys, one of them is 6 years old, you remind me of him."

"I am 7!" he said with all the indignation of a 7-year-old that has been miss-aged by an adult.

"Ohm, I should have guessed, you are way taller than my son!"

The child puffed up with pride.

"My name is Eliane. What is your name?"

"Ben."

"Nice to meet you, Ben. Would you come with me to the fires and have some more food? It's warm there and there's light."

"Not yet."

"No problem, we can stay here as long as you want."

"I'm hungry."

"Would you stay here with Milda while I get you food?"

A nod.

Ben relaxed as he ate and Eliane was able to learn more about him. He was a Dust Raider child, a human, that hasn't been long in Estuarius. He missed his family dearly, but they had not crossed over with him.

He said that they collected fruits that looked like coconuts, made a hole in them and filled them with a stinky drink then put a piece of fabric in the hole. The grown ups were lighting the fabric on fire and tossing the fruit. The sound scared him, so he ran away. He followed a pretty goat and made it through the crack in the mountain. He heard Eliane's group coming so he hid but then the monster broke the exit, and he could not go back to his grown ups. So, he decided to follow the Beautiful People instead.

"Beautiful People?" She asked.

"Yes, that is what the grown ups call them. And it's true, they are beautiful! But not you, you look like us!" he said with a smile.

"Yes" she said smiling, he really did remind her of her son and his blunt statements "Yes, I am also from Earth, like you."

"The Beautiful People are aliens?" he asked, eyes round.

"I don't know if they are aliens, but this place is called Estuarius. My friends are very nice. Are you ready to meet them?"

This time, he agreed.

Eliane was not prepared for the welcome she received. She had always seen the protective and friendly side of her companions. She was taken aback by the sudden change in the air. It somehow chilled. Conversation stopped completely as soon as she made it to the camp. Everywhere she looked, people were putting down drinks and reaching towards weapons. She met Faelan's eyes, she hadn't reached for anything, but she looked ready to spring, like a cat that spotted a dog getting close to her kittens. Ben felt it too, he hugged Eliane's leg and hid behind her. She could feel him trembling, so she put a hand on his shoulder for reassurance and hugged him tighter towards her. Milda jumped on his head, chattering disapprovingly.

Gary stepped out of the charged stillness which made Ben cower even more. The strong smell of urine betraying his fear "that is enough" Eliane said curtly. Gary stopped, surprised, while she scooped the child in her arms, not caring about his soiled clothes, only caring about keeping him safe and giving comfort.

Gary lifted both hands, palms out "peace Luimena, peace" he did no attempt at getting any closer. "Who is this Dust Raider pup that you are bringing to our camp?"

"This Earth child's name in Ben and he is with us now."

She may as well have tossed water to a grease fire. Eliane stared at Gary as everyone else spoke at once, she heard cries of "he's a spy" and "he's coming to poison us" and "check him for kokos."

This time, it was Faelan who stepped up. The group fell silent as she walked forward, stopping next to Gary, as a barrier. Eliane felt a wave of disappointment towards her friend. "Let's give him food and a place to sleep the night, then we will send him on his way, back to his people."

"We do not know where they are, he is lost" Eliane answered her.

They had finally left their weapons forgotten on the side, but the discontent was still obvious. They continued to try and dissuade her, but she was not going to take no for an answer "You need me to protect your world. He needs me to protect him. I am going to do both."

And that put an end to the argument.

The detour to the mountains had cost them a couple of extra days. The Kid, as Eliane's companions had started calling him, slept in the middle of the group cuddling her. He was afraid of the Beautiful People but trusted that she would keep him safe from them. The Dust Raiders had told him terrible stories about the people of Estuarius.

"Why are you so afraid of them?"

"The grown ups toled me they hate us and that is why they keep all the water for themselves. We have to go all the way to the river to grab water."

"Can they get water from the river?" Eliane asked him. Once he nodded, she continued "I would think that means that they are not stopping anyone from getting the water."

After a few moments of mulling her comment over, Ben continued "But Chief says that the Beautiful People don't let us have pipes. And that they keep us in the dark. They won't let us have electricity. They have light, we don't!"

"But Ben," she said kindly, "they don't actually have electricity because it hurts them." The Kid's eyes went as wide as they could go at those words. He looked worried. "Has the Chief ever tried to talk with the Beautiful People? It sounds to me like no one has tried to ask for help."

"I don't know. They told me to stay away because they will stop us from pogerezing." He sounded sad.

"Progressing?"

"Yes. And that they hurt us when they see us. They told me that they want to kill us because we are not beautiful like them."

Eliane had not noticed Faelan approaching them until she said, "who said you are not beautiful?"

Ben casted his eyes down with a shrug.

The Malauri kneeled down to be at his level "I think Eliane is beautiful, and I think you are beautiful too, don't you agree?"

He shrugged again but didn't move away from the woman's touch as he had done in the past. "My mom says I'm handsome, my dad calls me adorable."

Both women laughed with that answer. Faelan added, "you are very handsome."

"And strong" he said smiling and flexing his skinny arms."

"Yes, and strong!" Faelan said with a smile. After this, she switched into Malauri mode and decided to start teaching him how to know which herbs were good, which plants to avoid, and to never touch an animal. He seemed to love every single minute of it. Relishing in feeling useful when he collected tinder for their nightly fires.

The rest of the patrol took turns making up games and showing him different skills.

That day they decided to make camp early, well before night and Gary taught him how to light a fire safely.

When they were done having their dinner, Eliane picked up Ben and sat him on her lap as she watched the fire. He cuddled up to her, comfortable, he looked like a new child compared to the scared boy she had found just the night before. As they sat there, watching the fire, Ben turned his head and buried it on her hair. He had started to cry in silence.

Eliane let him cry, hugging him tight, stroking his hair. It was one of those healing cries that overwhelmed children needed to have. After a few minutes, he calmed down. With his head on her shoulder, he whispered "I want to go home, I want my mom and dad."

Eliane just kept stroking his hair and he continued "I don't want to go back to the other grown ups. They are all angry grown ups. I don't like that."

"You don't have to go anywhere. You can stay with me" she reassured him. He continued telling her how the Dust Raiders always complained about not having anything and how nobody ever wanted to play with him, calling him annoying. Afterwards, he told the story of crossing over to Estuarius and how he was calling for help. He said that the Chief took him and that when they were walking to the others, they found a box. He said the Chief started laughing when he saw it was filled with white things. "It's funny, he was so happy with the white things but he left one of them on a rainbow made of stone."

"Like this?" Gary interrupted. He had taken out a white earbud from an inside pocket and was holding it out to Ben.

"Yes!" He answered happily "That's the one!"

Gary stood up and offered Ben a hand "come, I will show you why the people of Estuarius are so afraid of Earth's technology."

They walked away from the camp, hand in hand, with Eliane walking alongside. Once they were further enough, Gary made a little doll with sticks and leaves. He then used a touch of magic to make it move. The little doll was walking smoothly in a little circle. Then Gary turned the earbud on and brought it close to the doll. The animated figure started walking slower, slower, slower, until it stopped, and with a shudder fell to the ground, inanimate once more.

Ben had been laughing and clapping at the doll. He had gotten quiet when the doll slowed down and he was now standing still, in stunned silence. He was looking at the doll with horror in his face.

Gary spoke again "the Beautiful People all have magic in

their bodies. That is what happens to them when their magic dies." He said pointing to the doll. "The technology from Earth kills the magic."

The Kid couldn't take it anymore and burst out crying, crying very loudly. Faelan and the rest of the group ran to where the trio was, ready to protect him. The sudden arrival cut Ben's tears short, and he looked between the group that had run to his rescue and the doll, laying motionless on the floor. He renewed his cries and between sobs he said, "I don't want that to happen."

Eliane went towards the group to explain what was happening so they could rest their defence. They lowered their arms and watched as Gary explained to the child "Neither do we, and that is why Eliane has to make it to the Arch of Renewal, so we can make sure the door between our worlds doesn't let the technology of yours wipe away this world."

Ben's cries stopped again, he wiped his nose on a very grubby sleeve and looked at the group that had come to his aid and solemnly he declared "I will help you."

As a unit, the group straightened up and hit their chest once with their fist. An acknowledgement of a promise made.

The rest of the evening was uneventful. The following day they kept teaching Ben different things. The Kid was an eager learner. His favourite thing to do was to climb trees to get fruits. It was during one of these climbs that he saw his previous group. He quickly reported it as soon as he made it to the ground. It was decided that Gary would visit the group with the child. They left Eliane behind for safety.

* * *

Gary could see that the group of Dust Raiders was afraid of him but Ben's presence, walking easily alongside him, somehow emboldened them. He would never understand why humans thought that a predator was less of a risk if a cub was present. The group's lack of magic was evident in their smell. They smelled empty, somehow.

He remained silent and unmoving while the cub told them what had happened since he last saw them. Not like they seemed any happier or relieved that he was alive. Ben told them what would happen if they stopped the Renewal. But their faces never changed, their smell remained the same, maybe a bit angrier.

"What do you know? You are just a kid!" said one of the raiders. Most of the angry aroma of the group seemed to be coming out of that particular human.

The cub seemed to shrink with the words. He started to shake and smelled of sadness.

"Eliane can help us, she's one of us! We can all live together!" Ben's courage to speak those words made Gary feel proud – *this cub is a leader.*

"The Beautiful People hate us!" That human was really angry, and what was that smell? Scared.

"No, they don't!!!" Ben shouted back and hugged Gary's leg. He picked the cub up and cuddled him in his arms with ease. He was holding onto his neck, his face buried, the spams of crying evident to anyone watching.

The angry human repeated himself, this time softly "What

would you know? You are just a kid" then to his comrades "he is just a kid."

Ben took his head out of Gary's neck and turned around to face the human. The cub's face was wet, and snot was running freely out of his nose. "They treat me right," he said through sobs, "they teach me things, they keep me warm, and give me food." He lowered his voice even more "they love me."

Something inside Gary broke and shifted. Nobody, and he meant nobody, was going to harm this cub anymore. Especially not that lump of wasted meat that spoke for the Dust Raiders. "You have seen me," he finally spoke. They all did a little surprised jump – *had they really forgotten that I was here?* – after the group nodded with a renewed wave of fear, he continued "Do you think I mean you harm?"

Nods.

"If I meant you harm, why didn't I kill you all at the crack in the mountain?"

Murmurs, everyone looking at each other, the smell of confusion strong in the air.

"Why have we cared for a child of Earth?"

More confused whispering.

"What would you do if a child of Estuarius showed up in your camp?"

Gary had not expected the words that came out of the group, they were angry yells of "spy!" and "kill him!"

Gary could feel hot rage building in his stomach and did not try to conceal it "So you are child murderers?" Ben renewed his cry, hugging him tighter, shaking so much he was almost vibrating. The Guider softened his voice only for the cub's sake and no one else's. "That is why the beautiful people, as you call them, fear you. Your capacity of harm. Your technology is a poison to them! And your way of thinking a weapon..." There was no anger anymore, it had been replaced by a profound sadness. Softly, he added "I will continue to defend the people. I will defend this world. And I will defend the Luimena. Our conversation is over" and he left, unafraid of attacks to his back, child cradled protectively in his arms.

*****

Eliane had been pacing nervously, waiting for Gary, worried for Ben. She was relieved to see him come back with The Kid in his arms. She had been afraid that the group of humans would claim him back.

They all listened attentively as Gary described his encounter with the Dust Raiders. Eliane sat on the side, with a happy Ben on her lap, he was playing with Milda while she absent mindedly caressed his hair. The news had made her so sad. She felt somehow defeated with the whole situation.

They broke camp and continued to their destination. Eyes alert, expecting an attack at any moment.

Eliane's group should not have bothered with all the vigilance. They were never going to be ambushed. The Dust Raiders were waiting for them at the Arch of Renewal. She was expecting the actual arch to look just like the arches that were supposed to be her original landing place. Instead, she could see one large arch hovering above the hostile group, its big stones covered in moss and vines. It was an imposing structure that radiated age.

The group of disheveled humans were blocking their access to the monument. They had the look of determination of those willing to die for their cause.

The two groups faced each other, making sure to leave a healthy distance in between. Both unwilling to take the first step. Eliane decided to break the stalemate "Please move aside! We just want to get to the Arch!" she called out and was answered by a chorus of "traitor" and "never!"

Once the screams had died down, a man at the front said "why should we help you? You are clearly one of us, but you are helping the Beautiful People instead!"

"Hi! I'm Eliane. I don't want any trouble." She said with a smile, trying to diffuse the situation.

But the man would not allow her to say anything. Someone from the group behind him mustered enough courage and threw a rock at Eliane. She didn't even have a chance to bring her arms to her face when Faelan threw a disk that broke the rock into dust. The Malauri took a second to wink at her friend before turning back to face the Dust Raiders. The human group broke rank and started running towards the imposing arch as a single man ran towards the locals. The sole attacker had the hood of his dirty sweater up and covering his face "it's the Tech Golem!" someone in her group yelled, and they braced themselves. The lone human hands came out of his sweater's pockets with a fistful of earbuds which he threw at the magical group as soon as he was in range. He then turned around and went back to reunite with his people.

The effect was immediate. All around Eliane people started feeling sick. Ben scurried through the feet of his dizzy friends, collecting as many of the offending electronics as he could. One of the groups shot an arrow at the retreating figure but in his dizziness, he missed the shot. Eliane's cries of "stop! Please stop!" were ignored and her companions rushed towards the human with cries of battle in their lips.

Gary scooped Ben up and ran away from the fight, protecting the child from any errant projectile.

Eliane watched in dismay as the Dust Raiders, using kokos, broke down the arch moments before her friends were able to meet them. The sound of the structure collapsing seemed to get louder and louder. Eliane did not understand how she could still hear it, and hear it ever more intensively now that the rocks were all resting on the ground. It was deafening. Everyone stopped and looked up. Eliane followed their gaze – *it's a freaking dragon! A real-life dragon!* – An impossibly big black beast had appeared out of nowhere. With a giant roar, the dragon shot hot blue flames over everyone. They were high enough over their heads that the flames didn't hurt anyone but low enough that they could feel their heat.

The dragon flapped its wings slowly, getting ready for a soft landing. The sound like a giant tent loose in the wind. Dead branches, debris, and dust all raging around the panicked people. Everyone was running away for their life without a care of their planet of origin.

Eliane, however, was not moving. She was transfixed by the scene. Her dreams had come true, it was a real dragon! She was in the presence of a real dragon! Faelan grabbed her face in both her hands, breaking eye contact, and told her to run. They ran towards the forest when the ground shook, indicating that the dragon had landed. Eliane stopped and turned around to look at it. The black behemoth let out another loud roar, wings at its sides. As the dust settled, a small voice from the back of the dragon called out "are you all done with the stupid fight? I want to go home!" and off the shoulder of the dragon pops out none other but Ben. The Kid continued "the renewal WILL HAPPEN, humans, stand aside or be eaten!" Dragon moved his giant head towards the Dust Raiders, and they cowered in the ruins of the arches. The dragon blew a derisible smoky air through the nose at them.

"No!" Eliane screamed, "do not eat anyone!" The dragon turned its giant head towards Eliane and cocked it to the side, like a dog. The gesture reminded her of Doggie and its eyes… "Gary?" The dragon chuckled. Never did she ever imagine the sound of a dragon chuckling. It was a rich sound from deep inside like a rockslide that sounded happy.

The dragon – *oh my god Gary is a dragon!* – lowered his head all the way to the ground and Ben hopped down from it, ran towards Eliane, and hugged her. She started crying happy tears, and spoke loudly so everyone could hear "Don't you see? Everyone is afraid because no one understands anything! Estuarius people are afraid of the dragon but it's just Guider!" They started to come out slowly. "The people from Earth are afraid of everything because it's a strange world. We are all scared of the unknown, but this place is full of beauty and magic, good magic!"

Someone yelled "it's not home!"

Eliane yelled back "and you didn't try to make it home! Have you learned NOTHING from our shared history?! You came in trying to kill, to destroy! Why haven't you tried to understand your surroundings? To look at the beauty? To integrate?! Now, I do not know how long you all have been here, but time is different so it may not be that long on Earth. It's June, it's June 2023."

Her words caused as much surprise among the Dust Raiders as the dragon had. They all started talking to themselves. She could hear "so little time has passed" and "but we've been stuck here for months" and "I've been here for years!". A shout "what does it matter if we can't go back?"

"Who said you cannot?!" They were not expecting that.

Eliane turned to Gary, still in dragon form "Could you bring them back? You once told me you bring back the ones that cross over to Earth, could you do the same for the Dust Raiders?"

"Yes" he said in his booming draconic voice.

"You can go back!" Eliane repeated to the group of defeated humans.

Some started to cry, "my family, I will be able to see my family" another "my dog must be missing me" and also "I want to use a toilet again!" people laughed among their tears.

Someone, a man, broke through and said "what if you don't want to go back? There's nothing for me back on Earth but debt and depression. I have a family here."

"Stay with us!" said a voice from among her companions and Eliane could recognize that melodic voice, like butter on warm bread. Faelan continued "we will teach you our ways, we can help you build and live here."

The same man explained that they actually had a settlement in some ruins, and he had a pregnant wife there "she is a third-generation settler. She did not want us to stop you. The ones that stayed behind didn't believe in the fight."

The talks continued about going to the human settlement and offering passage back to Earth to those who wanted. Also, of rebuilding among those who wanted to stay. They spoke about posts along the belt to help the transition for those who find themselves on this side of the belt. Gary went back to the form Eliane had gotten to know so well – *when did he do that?* – and said that he could speak with his clan to serve as liaison and bring back those who needed it "my daughter could do with the practice" he said.

# | 6 |

# The Act of Renewal

It had always been a quiet ceremony, just the Guider alone with the Luimena. This was the first time Estuarians would be present.

The arch was never needed, it only just marked the location. Together, the Dust Raiders and the Beautiful People, sifted through the rubble and, with the pieces salvaged from it, they made a circle where the arch used to be.

Once the circle was built, everyone took a step back to admire their work in silence. Gary grabbed Eliane's hand on his own and brought her to the center of the ring while everyone stood just around it, surrounding them. "Ready?" Gary asked her, "ready" she replied with a smile. This was it; this is what she was meant to do, this would save a world, maybe even two. Her eyes watered with emotion at the enormity of what was about to happen, at the role she was about to play in something that was so much bigger than her and those she knew and got to love.

Gary smiled back, understanding the meaning of her unshed tears. He held both her hands and started making a low deep bass sound, like a resonance. First, she felt a tingling where he was touching her, soon, it started spreading up her arms until she could feel it all over her body. It was not unpleasant. He started to modify the cadence of his low resonance up and down and she felt her blood respond to it until he reached the height of the crescendo. He held the note until she felt like ants were inside her veins. When she could not hold it any longer, he took out a pin from the inside of his dark jacket, his song cut off abruptly as he made a small puncture on her upturned finger.

The memory of the resonance lingered in the air, waiting as blood pooled on the puncture. A single drop floated up, and a very quiet hum, like an echo of Gary's song, seemed to be coming out of it, the ruby drop vibrating in tune. The drop continued to vibrate and started to rotate, the hum enveloped everything and then the single drop seemed to explode with a sound like a sigh of relief. From that point, a warm light started radiating, converging into the very center of the circle, from there it started swirling, like being sucked into a pipe – *it's going into the belt!* – From there, the light spread out like a tide coming to shore. It now surrounded everything, a big shield of orange hue, enveloping all of Estuarius. All the colours now seemed brighter, richer. Gary turned to the spectators and simply said "it is done" and everyone cheered.

| 7 |

# A New Time

They finally arrived at the Dust Raiders' settlement, Eliane could see from the distance that it was, indeed, some old ruins they had taken for themselves. "People moved out of that town when I was but a child. They resettled in Moss-brook for a more strategic place for their de-salting process" commented Gary.

Although it was old ruins, the place was not in ruins. It looked clean and well tended. Roofs had been fixed with branches and straw. Streets were free of debris and the humans were clean. There was a patch of farmland and a pen with animals that looked like goats. Their horns would not have looked out of place on a moose, though – *I would hate to be the one to milk one of those* – All in all, it had the air of a peaceful little village. Before they got any closer, Eliane turned to Gary and complained "you know, you told me that I was going to see unicorns, and the last thing I ever saw was a unicorn!"

Ben started to giggle "oh, oh, they are behind that hill! They are behind that hill! Come!" and he dragged her with all the strength of an excited little boy.

As soon as they topped the hill, Eliane's breath caught in her lungs. On the valley below them, was a huge blessing of unicorns. There were so many she didn't even try to count them. She could see all the colours of the rainbow represented in pastel hues. Everywhere she looked, she could see a different colour, she saw yellow, lilac, blue, green, golden, silver, peach, salmon, pink, grey, teal, and white. Their shiny manes one or two shades more vibrant than their bodies. Their pointy horns seemed to reflect the light like a mirror hidden in the tall grass.

Ben put his arm around Eliane's waist, and she rested her arm on his shoulders, both quietly watching the magical group existing peacefully. After a few minutes of quiet contemplation, he mischievously said, "look at this" and he let out the loudest "whoop!" his little lungs could muster.

What happened next would forever remain one of Eliane's favourite memories of her adventure. The whole blessing did a little startled hop in unison, and then they all took off in the same direction, as a unit, following the leader of the group. She wasn't the biggest animal, but she was clearly in charge. Her golden mane was streaked with silver strands, and it billowed in the wind while she ran. She neighed loudly, making sure everyone knew where to go and took the rest of the blessing away, into the forest. The thunder of their hooves making the ground vibrate under the spectators' feet. Eliane could follow their progress even when she could no longer see them through the trees, as flocks of birds would take flight when the magnificent animals grew near them.

"Wow" was all Eliane could say.

"I know, right?" the child giggled again. They went back to where they had left Gary.

He told them that the humans that wanted to go back to Earth, had started to organize themselves. They were to wait for Gary's clan in order to coordinate their trip back. "They should be here tomorrow at first light."

"How?" Eliane interrupted him. "Everything we have done has taken forever, messages sent by foot, everyone walks, no one rides anything. How do they know to come here and how would they do it so fast?"

Gary laughed, gave her the laconic answer of "magic" and winked at her. And that was all the explanation she would get about that particular topic.

They walked into the settlement. Chief welcomed them alongside his pregnant wife. He then invited Faelan to tour the place with them.

"My job here is done" Eliane said to her friend. She was really going to miss having her in her life. "It's time for me to go back to my family."

They hugged, trying to convey as much love as possible through the gesture. With a sad smile, Eliane gave Milda back to her friend "I also wanted you to be the one to have my vambraces, to keep you safe while you keep your shoes" Faelan laughed at the words shand took the furball and the arm braces with a smile. She then got serious and took her friends' hands in her own "Thank you for everything, and for giving me back sisterly love. My life had been so empty since my sister left and you have filled it back. And now we have more friends" she said, extending her arm towards the Dust Raiders encampment. "You have redefined life as we know it. I will never forget you!" They hugged again, this time with tears in their eyes. Eliane watched her go with Chief towards the settlement. She turned to Gary, picked up The Kid in her arms and declared "I'm ready!"

"Yeah, you are not going back with Ben."

"But! I promised him that I was going to bring him back safely!" she argued.

"Yes, I will do that, I can get him exactly to the city he belongs to, or do you think he lives in your neighbourhood?"

"I hadn't thought of that" Eliane confessed.

He laughed, "of course not, and that's alright. I will bring him to the police station nearest to his house and leave. No one will be able to ask me questions. Imagine? You could be accused of kidnapping! We don't need that drama!"

Giggling, she replied "I really had not thought that far ahead."

"He'll come with us to drop you off and I'll take it from there."

He waved a hand and the familiar silver line appeared, it stretched and there it was: her way home.

# | 8 |

# Home

Eliane was standing on her driveway, looking at her home. She turned to look at Gary, and with a smile, gave him a kiss on the warm cheek "say hi to my grand or great kids from me. I'll never forget you, and I'll make sure they will look for you or your daughter". Eliane then turned to Ben and gave him a big hug before turning back towards her house. She was nervous, it had been a bit over two weeks since she last saw them but only 17 hours for her family. She looked back again but her friends were already gone. She took a deep calming breath and walked through her door.

Eliane was in her house – *finally, home!* – and she was welcomed by the familiar sounds of food making, laughing, and too loud cartoons. She knelt as soon as she saw Doggie running to receive her. He smashed against her with lots of face licking as her sweet boys ran over to give her a hug, – *can life be any better?* – Feeling like her soul was complete once more, she lifted her head and saw her husband, looking at her with inquiring eyes, she nodded at him with a secret smile that promised him a long chat later "Mom? Where were you? Mommy, you stink!"

Tairy Diaz Gil is a happy mom of two, living her life where the wind hurts her face. She is a forever fanatic of dogs and dragons in no particular order.